Stranded with My Mafia Boss

A Kinky Billionaire Age Gap

Marrying the Mob

Book One

Cora Masters

Stranded with My Mafia Boss

© Copyright 2023 Cora Masters

Published by The Phantom Pen

Cover by Glowing Moon Designs

Formatting by The Phantom Pen

 Created with Vellum

To all who've had a hot-as-hell boss and couldn't do jack about it. Live vicariously.

Damien

The model lay sprawled across my bed, toned limbs askew and golden hair fanned out around her head like a halo.

I couldn't remember her name. It was something ridiculous, like Wolf or Panther or Rabbit. She had a nice figure, slender with large man-made tits, but her conversation bored me to absolute fucking tears.

On the plus side, she could suck the chrome off a trailer hitch. A task I might set her to again if she didn't shut the fuck up.

Rabbit got up and put a robe on. I had insisted she be clothed outside of the bedroom. While my body-guards might've enjoyed the show, I had my limits.

Even if this woman was mine for only a few hours, she was still mine alone for that time.

"Daaamien," she whined, drawing out each syllable of my name. The sound grated at my nerves, but it was second nature to keep the irritation from my face. "I'm dying for a cup of real coffee. A proper one, not that rubbish your bodyguard made."

I waved a hand in the general direction of the door, eager to be rid of her inane blather. "There's a grinder and coffee pot in the kitchen. Help yourself."

She pouted, sticking out her collagen-enhanced bottom lip. "I only drink fresh roasted Finca El Injerto coffee. My staff picks it up from the farm in Guatemala. It's the only kind worth drinking."

I pinched the bridge of my nose and sighed. An idea began to form in my mind, a way to speed up this entire tedious process. I reached for my phone on the bedside table, scrolling through my contacts until I found my PA's number.

She picked up on the second ring. "Mr. Santini? How may I help you?" Katie's voice was brisk and professional, as always. I imagined her sitting ramrod straight behind her desk, red hair tucked in a bun, a faintly nervous gleam in her eye.

She'd been an accountant before she'd discovered illegal transactions in one of my shell companies, and instead of simply having her killed, I'd made her my personal assistant. My actions had made my cousin, the don of the Montrelli family, comment that I'd gotten soft in my old age.

The day I let his opinion dictate my actions would be a cold one in hell, indeed. Which reminded me. I needed to send a new phone to his daughter Bria. It had been long enough her old one would have had spyware installed in it while she wasn't looking.

I preferred my conversations with my favorite niece to be unmonitored.

"Miss Jones, I have two urgent errands for you. First, send a new smartphone to Bria Montrelli, by the usual drop location. Then I need you to fly to Guatemala immediately after to pick up a few pounds of fresh roasted Finca El Injerto coffee and then bring it straight to my cabin in Aspen." I kept my tone serious, hiding my amusement at the ridiculousness of the request.

There was a beat of silence and then, "I apologize sir, but that doesn't seem feasible. It's Friday and I'm on vacation for Christmas all next week. I can have them ship—"

"This is not a request. I expect you on a plane to Guatemala and back to my cabin by this evening. Use the private jet. Do I make myself clear?"

She hesitated for only a moment. "Yes, perfectly clear. I will make the arrangements immediately." The line went dead as she hung up. The days of slamming the receiver down were over, but I sensed the intent.

I turned back to the supermodel, scrutinizing her body. "You're in luck. My assistant is off to get your coffee. In the meantime, why don't you show some appreciation?"

The model, Foxx, oh yes, that was her name, widened her eyes as some emotion managed to work its way through her brain. Maybe fear, maybe greed, I neither knew nor cared.

She didn't protest, and I gave her credit for how gracefully she fell to her knees. My cock in her mouth let her showcase her talents. With her tongue swirling and her fingers caressing my balls, I should have come faster, but I was oddly dissatisfied. Gazing down, I imagined her hair red.

There we were. Hands in her hair, I thrust hard, eyes closed. Yes, red hair, curves...I spurted hard and fast into Foxx's mouth.

Foxx coughed and then gagged toward the end, not that it had slowed me down, and I patted her ass when she got up. "That was great. Foxx. Not gonna lie."

Greed shone in her eyes. I'd have to give her the diamond necklace I'd picked up to pay her with early, just to help boot her out of the cabin.

I didn't really want her, after all.

When we headed downstairs for lunch, I took Alex aside. One of my bodyguards, he was also plugged into the social scene and could deliver what I needed: Foxx gone in a plausible fashion, rather than kicking her out.

"Get Foxx an invite to Richard McCord's Christmas party in L.A. I want her out of here by this evening."

Rich McCord, a business acquaintance of mine, had his latest divorce finalized a week ago and he was looking for hookups. Foxx was on the prowl to marry a rich man, so she'd jump for the opportunity, especially since I'd made it plain that I had no intention of becoming her meal ticket.

Alex nodded and retreated with his phone. My other bodyguard, Rico, pulled out salad greens and leftover roast chicken from the fridge.

"Just salad for me, no dressing," said Foxx.

About halfway through lunch, Foxx's phone pinged, and her blue eyes rounded when she read the text.

Success.

Then she glanced at me. After looking blank for a moment, she smiled.

So many teeth there. Very white. Unnaturally so.

"Damien, I have an offer for a shoot, I'm so sorry. I'm going to have to go. The model who was doing it got sick, but I have to leave right now and get to the flight. Could you be a dear and have one of your men drive me?"

Coming up with that story on the fly must have taken her real effort. No lines to be fed or photographer to tell her exactly which way to look. I might had been impressed if I cared.

I debated resisting for a moment, just to be annoying, then realized it might intimidate her into staying. "Of course. Why don't you pack now, and Rico and Alex will take you to the airport as soon as you're ready."

When she came down again, I handed her the gift-wrapped package, and she kissed me before leaving in a flurry of more kisses blown from her fingertips and a near mountain of designer luggage.

After they left, I texted both Alex and Rico that they could take the rest of the week off and go back home to Boston. After a short argument, they returned to ensure the security system was armed and the arsenal was fully stocked. They informed me that they'd be staying in town, not going to Boston, and drove off, leaving me alone with my thoughts.

Katie Jones should show up here tomorrow. There was no way she'd made it by tonight like I'd demanded.

I leaned back on the sofa, closing my eyes and picturing her in my mind. That fiery mane of red hair all bundled in a braided bun, those emerald eyes that told me to fuck myself while that lovely mouth stammered platitudes, the soft curve of her hips and breasts. She exuded an aura of mature sensuality, and just the mere thought of her sent a surge of desire through me.

Normally I dated tall, leggy blondes, creatures like Foxx who asked no questions and made no demands and were fine with subbing in exchange for luxury gifts.

Katie, on the other hand, was intelligent, strong-willed, and maddeningly cheerful. She'd find a silver lining in the darkest cloud.

She was also blissfully unaware of her undeniable attraction. In the year since she'd come to work with me, the crackle of energy in her presence had left me unsettled and on edge. I wanted to break that sweet exterior and unleash the passion simmering just below the surface. To dominate her completely and make her surrender.

To me.

All I needed was privacy and a little time without distractions, like now.

The idea of having Katie at my mercy, of taking her in every way imaginable, was intoxicating. My cock throbbed in anticipation, and I gritted my teeth.

This little game of mine might prove more dangerous than I had anticipated, but fuck, the rewards would be oh, so sweet when she consented.

And she would consent. I would make sure of it.

In a conflict between cheerfulness and passion, I would make sure passion won. By the time I was finished with her, Katie would beg for more.

I HUNG UP THE PHONE, CURSING UNDER MY breath. Why couldn't my boss be a *regular* billionaire with normal requests? No, I had to work for a mafia kingpin who sent me on wild goose chases around the globe. Leave Boston to get coffee from Guatemala then deliver it to him on vacation in Aspen? Seriously?

It hadn't started this way. My degree was in accounting. I'd started taking college classes my junior year in high school, since, Mother had already been hinting she'd be leaving soon. It was hard, but I'd graduated from college in record time and got a real job with a holding company just after my twenty-first birthday. My brother had the insurance he needed, and we had enough money to get by.

I'd worked for the company for three years before I started finding discrepancies and brought it up to my supervisor, and when he did nothing, I took it to his manager.

Long story short, I'd ended up standing in front of the big boss and a couple of guys who looked like they enjoyed chewing nails and spitting out bullets. The phrase 'an offer you can't refuse' applied to my reassignment and I became the assistant to the big boss. From accountant to PA. What a step down in resume but a massive step up in pay. I was now the one who handled the unusual aspects of Damien's business empire. The part where the criminal organization interfaced with it.

My very first task had been fixing the accounting that had made me suspicious.

At least the pay was good, and while my boss had all the warmth of a glacier in a snowstorm, the health insurance covered most of Max's needs. My younger brother had a chronic autoimmune disease, and treatment was expensive. He'd just turned eighteen and started college, so I hoped he'd get a job with good insurance when he graduated.

Getting this position, however accidental and perilous, had put us in the best place we'd been since Mom left when I turned eighteen. Enough money, so I just tried *really hard* not to think about what might happen if I got caught. It wasn't like I could do much about it anyway.

In the meantime, I sucked it up and did the work. I'd been afraid I'd have to deal with harming people, but my job ended up being making sure the money went where it was supposed to go, making appointments with scary people in badly fitted suits to meet with allies and competitors, and weird little jobs like getting coffee from other countries.

Which was actually kind of cool when it wasn't the freakin' week before Christmas.

Luckily the company jet was free. I kept a carry-on at work for these *emergencies*. I was a fool me once kind of gal, and the third time he'd pulled a stunt like this, I'd been prepared. Take that, stone-faced Santini.

Now the hard part.

I called Max and got his voicemail. He was in class. "I've got to make a quick trip. I should be back the day after tomorrow. Stay out of the presents and I'll see you as soon as I can. I'll have Connor check on you."

Then I texted Connor O'Hara, our next-door neighbor. He was an artist, working from home, and a seriously nice guy.

> Can you keep an eye on Max?
> Emergency business trip, might
> take 2 days.

> Sure.

It was just me and Max, Dad died when Max was a baby, and I worried if I had to leave my little brother alone for a long time. He'd had flare-ups come up with no warning, and they made him sick enough that he couldn't do much for himself.

With everything important sorted, I embarked on my new adventure. I spoke enough Spanish to get by, and sunny warm Guatemala should be a treat after the ice and snow in Boston this past week.

Well, once I got there, at least it was sunny, but a bumpy ride. Arriving just before dawn, I set off in a rental car.

I'd used internet searches to find the farm, but it was a three-hour drive from where I landed. My usual business wear was conservative enough not to cause any problems with the locals, but I still got catcalls as I rented a car and plotted my route to the highlands of Huehuetenango. Bumpy roads, winding paths, and the air conditioner giving up the ghost made the drive out less than fun.

I'd slept on the plane, so driving through the morning and a gorgeous sunrise was pleasant. The scenery was gorgeous, and the people were kind when I got to the farm, offering me lunch. Bean tostadas and something called chuchitos which were like little tamales and *delicious*. They also had a special fruit punch they said was made only around Christmas.

I bought a few pounds of the five hundred-dollar-a-pound coffee to prevent a trip in the near future. With two of the silver and black bags tucked in my carry-on, I started back to the city, certain I would make my flight. I had plenty of time.

EXHAUSTION MADE ME MOVE LIKE MY PUFFY blue down coat was made of bricks as I picked my way up the path to the cabin—AKA *mansion*—nestled in the mountains. With the weather turning bad, my ten-hour flight had expanded to twenty with delays and diversions.

Now I was here, finally, exhausted, starving, and cold with the packages of coffee, my carry-on, and a reservation at a local motel once I dropped this package off. I still had a couple of days left until Christmas. I'd rebooked my flight back to Boston for tomorrow just in case. I was asleep on my feet, no way I was going back tonight.

The things I did for this asshole. He'd better believe I was going to put in for all the expenses, too.

I'd texted Alex, one of the bodyguards, on the way in. So I should've been expected and could hand the coffee off and then hit the hotel.

I pressed the doorbell, counting the seconds until I could scuttle back to the taxi and head for my nice warm room with a nice soft mattress.

Even exhaustion from the long journey couldn't keep me from marveling at the stunning scenery surrounding me. Tall, snow-covered pines framed the huge luxurious log cabin, which was far more grandiose than any cabin had a right to be.

The door opened, revealing another bit of stunning scenery. Even though he was my boss, Damien Santini was hot as the sun—if you liked dark, brooding older men. Which apparently, some part of me did. I had to look up to meet his gaze, but then, I had to look up to most people.

Tall and broad-shouldered, Damien had chiseled cheekbones, a cleft chin, and black hair swept back. His eyes, vivid blue, were colder than the wind working its way into my coat. It was unfair that a man in his mid-forties could look that good, and worse than that I was always attracted to older men. Not that I ever acted on it.

The coldness of his expression helped keep me from drooling. The air of menace helped too. The man never smiled, as far as I knew.

"Miss Jones," he said with his usual crisp tone, gaze sweeping up and down my frazzled, puffy-coated self. "You're late."

"Apologies, Mr. Santini." I forced a smile, trying to maintain my professional demeanor as I handed him the bag. "Here's the coffee."

"Foxx has already left. It seems you've come all this way for nothing."

My patience snapped. All that effort, a two-day-long grueling journey, for what? A snippy comment? I tried not to let my annoyance show. "I can't control the storm or the air traffic controllers. Perhaps if you'd sent someone to threaten the weather, I would have gotten here earlier."

So much for not letting the annoyance show. I bit my lip to keep any more words from falling out.

"True." He ignored the snippy comment, his gaze on mine. He broke eye contact and waved dismissively at the cab. The cab driver, perhaps sensing my imminent doom, hurriedly left, tires crunching in the snow.

Damien stared down at me. "Miss Jones, you will stay here tonight."

Not what I wanted, but with the cab gone, I didn't have much choice. Once again, Damien wanted twenty-four-seven service and maneuvered me to get it.

I glanced at the sky. Throughout the taxi ride, I'd watched the dark clouds gathering as the sun began to set. Another storm was brewing. If my luck kept up as it had been this last day, I'd be stranded in Damien's cabin with nothing but my carry-on and a pile of work he'd no doubt produce from nowhere. My mind raced, weighing my options. I could try to find another cab, but was it worth it?

My instincts screamed for me to refuse, to put as much distance between myself and this dangerous man as possible. They'd been yelling since that scary interview a year ago.

The cold wind bit at the exposed skin of my face and slithered through my coat. What choice did I have? At least I'd get to see the inside of the cabin. If it matched the outside, it must be gorgeous. "Thank you, Mr. Santini. I appreciate the offer. I need some downtime. I haven't slept in over a day. My flight is tomorrow, and I am now technically on vacation, remember?"

Sometimes it was hard to keep the irony out of my tone.

"Come in." He opened the door and gestured for me to enter. "Please, call me Damien. Do you prefer Katherine or Katie?"

His voice was different, almost inviting. It gave me goosebumps that had nothing to do with the cold.

"Katie, uh, *Damien*," I said, still trying to maintain some semblance of professionalism. My heart thumped. A part of me was intrigued by this sudden welcome, a side of him I'd never seen before.

A very silly part of me.

When I stepped into the cabin, warm air surrounded me like a hug. Oh, yes.

"Make yourself at home," Damien said, his gaze never leaving mine. "There's a ready guest room at the top of the stairs on the right. If you need anything, text me. Alex and Rico are away, so we're alone right now."

Alone? He was *never* alone. Not that I'd ever seen.

"Erm, thank you," I said, acutely aware of his closeness. Then I headed for the stairs as fast as my tired feet would take me. They gleamed with polish, a rich dark brown.

When I opened the door to the guest room the light came on automatically. I sucked in an appreciative breath. The king-sized bed with plush pillows and a velvet duvet beckoned my tired achy self. Floor-to-ceiling windows framed a breathtaking view of a snow-covered landscape. The amber gleam of polished wood floors in the warm light cast by a crystal chandelier was a balm on my tired eyes.

"Wow," I muttered under my breath, setting down my old off-brand carry-on on the bed. The duvet didn't spontaneously throw it across the room, which was good.

The siren song of the shower pulled me in first. Once the warm jets of water and scented creamy soaps were done having their way with me, my stomach growled hard.

Wrapped in the world's plushest towel, I checked the closet. There was a variety of clothes in it, and after a quick search, I found an ugly Christmas sweater and a set of leggings that fit.

This place wasn't decorated for Christmas at all. How odd.

My stomach snarled at me again, so I went exploring for food. At this point, just about anything would taste good.

From the top of the stairs, I sniffed appreciatively and then followed the aroma of garlic. The kitchen wasn't far from the entry area, and I stopped dead in my tracks, staring at Damien as he stood over the stove, expertly flipping a pan full of what appeared to be shrimp scampi.

"Damien?" I raised my eyebrows in surprise. "You cook?"

He looked over, face as grim as usual. There was a gleam in his eyes, though... "Surprised?"

"A bit." This was a side of him I'd never seen before. Also, the smell was making me want to drool.

He tapped his phone and music started to play. A lovely piano piece, I recognized the music. "You like Andrea Stewart too?"

I had all her music on my lists at home. She played with a passion I loved.

"Yes, I enjoy her music. Go ahead, have a seat." He gestured toward the kitchen table, the pale wood already set with gleaming silverware and creamy glazed stoneware. Hesitantly, I pulled out a chair and sat down, watching him as he moved with brisk ease around the kitchen.

The music glided into a slower pace, and I relaxed

listening to it, tension seeping out of my tired muscles. The woman had a real artistic gift.

Speaking of which, the question popped out of my mouth. "Why do you know how to cook?"

"Hard to be poisoned if you cook your own food," he said offhandedly. "You know, things in my world can get tense."

Completely inappropriately, my stomach rumbled loud enough to be heard across the kitchen.

"Eat," Damien said, placing a plate piled high with shrimp scampi in front of me. The aroma was mouth-watering, and my stomach growled again in anticipation.

I took a bite and then stuffed another in my mouth. It was delicious.

Damien poured Pinot Grigio and set a glass next to me. Then he placed his own plate and glass next to mine rather than across the table. Busy inhaling the food, I didn't comment. I didn't care. At that second, he could've murdered someone in front of me, as long as I kept my plate.

When the edge of my hunger tampered off, I gave

credit where it was due. "This is delicious. I had no idea you were such a good cook."

"Many people are surprised by what I can do," he sipped his wine. "How was Guatemala?"

"Beautiful." I took another bite of the tender shrimp. "It's also a bit strange. Like any time you visit a place for the first time. I'll admit, I was worried when I had to get to the airport at night. All the guidebooks said women shouldn't travel alone at night. Lots of Christmas decorations, though."

"It's good to follow warnings. Every place has its dark side, Katie," he said, his voice low and intense. "As for decorating, good for them."

"What do you have against decorating?" I asked, trying to inject a little humor. He'd never been so personal with me before, and it was making me nervous, but at the same time, it made excitement fizzle in my, erm, lower belly. Very low.

"Waste of time." Damien spoke in that dark and dangerous voice, even though the conversation was trivial.

I took refuge in the food, eating another shrimp. And another. Once I finished chewing, I continued,

"It was an adventure. It'll be great to go back some-time when I have more time to explore."

He nodded, watching me eat over his wine glass.

Silence reigned for the rest of the meal. Beneath it all, there was an undercurrent, one that made me nervous just as much as it intrigued me.

I yawned, the last bit of pasta stuffing me and setting me on a path to bed. "Sorry, I'm tired. See you in the morning?"

"Certainly," My boss watched me as I rose, gaze lingering.

"Goodnight," I said, unsure whether to be grateful or terrified for his hospitality.

"Goodnight, Katie," he said, smooth and controlled, as always. "Sleep well."

How did he make that sound so inviting? Almost lewd.

Climbing the stairs to the guest room, my thoughts swirled like the snowflakes just outside the window. The evening had been nothing short of surreal. I'd seen a side of Damien Santini that made me want to know him better, which was just this side of suicidal.

Outside my window, the snow came down thick and fast, piling up. Several new inches had fallen, and the storm was still going strong.

Tiredness mugged me. I needed to sleep so badly it wasn't funny, and the food in my stomach was doing its best to put me in a carb coma.

"Get a grip, Katie," I muttered, shaking off my worries and stepping into the room.

When I pulled back the duvet, the scent of lavender filled the air. The rich ivory silken sheets whispered seductively against my skin as I pulled them back.

Despite the storm raging outside, the room was warm and inviting, lit only by soft, glowing lamps.

I changed into a t-shirt, strangely vulnerable as I slipped between the cool, luxurious sheets and used the remote on the nightstand to turn off the lights.

The pale glow from the security lights on the snow gave the room just enough illumination to keep me from tripping if I used the bathroom during the night.

Snuggling into the pillows, thoughts popped up like gophers despite my extreme exhaustion. What if Damien tried something? What if he came into my room while I slept? Then, a bad influence in the back of my head said, would that be so terrible?

"Stop it," I scolded myself, pressing a hand to my forehead. No thoughts in that direction, nope.

The wind howled against the window, a puff of snow splatting down from the trees.

I turned on my side and gazed out the window at the snowstorm. From a nice warm bedroom, it was pretty to watch. Like Damien from a safe distance.

Did I want to keep my distance?

With that unsettling question lingering in my mind, sleep rolled over me.

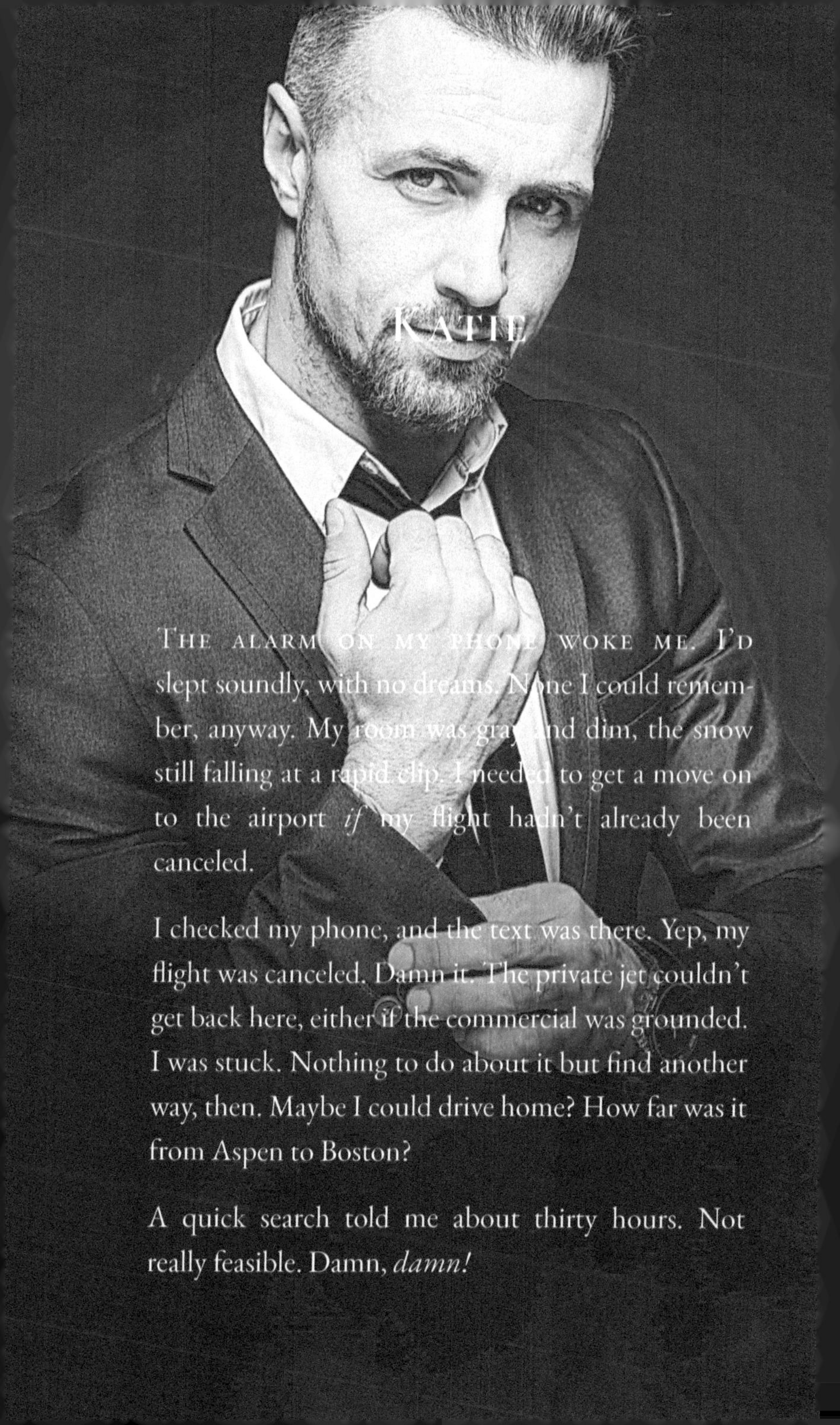

The alarm on my phone woke me. I'd slept soundly, with no dreams. None I could remember, anyway. My room was gray and dim, the snow still falling at a rapid clip. I needed to get a move on to the airport *if* my flight hadn't already been canceled.

I checked my phone, and the text was there. Yep, my flight was canceled. Damn it. The private jet couldn't get back here, either if the commercial was grounded. I was stuck. Nothing to do about it but find another way, then. Maybe I could drive home? How far was it from Aspen to Boston?

A quick search told me about thirty hours. Not really feasible. Damn, *damn!*

As I typed out a message to my brother, I swung my legs over the side of the bed. I was still a little stiff from all the time in airplane seats, but sleep had taken care of most of it.

After a quick shower and a mental note to find where the laundry was in this place, I put on my last pair of clean underwear and another outfit from the closet, this one a long sleeve, button-down silky shirt, and jeans. The shirt had Kiss Me spelled out in cursive glitter on the single pocket over my left breast.

Ugh. I understood why whoever had abandoned it. The shirt was the only other warm thing that really fit me, though. Most of the clothes were too big.

The scent of freshly brewed coffee pulled me down the grand staircase and into the kitchen.

"Good morning," Damien said, already by the griddle with a steaming mug in one hand and a spatula in the other. The five-hundred-dollars-a-pound Guatemalan coffee bag sat by the fancy coffee maker. I ignored a small thrill as I poured myself a cup. At least I got to drink what I'd gone to such lengths to acquire.

Damien quirked an eyebrow. "We are officially snowed in."

"Mmm," I muttered under my breath as I took my first sip. Snowed in with my mobster boss. Sounded like a steamy romance novel to me.

Down girl, focus. No doubt Damien was going to use the time to change my vacation to work from home on a mountain. He wasn't issuing an invitation for sexytimes.

I was going to claw my vacation back from him, too. No way was I going to spend this time working and not get my vacay back. He'd have to give me the week after Christmas instead.

"Breakfast?" Damien asked, gesturing toward the stove where pancakes and bacon sizzled.

It smelled good but looked like it would set heavy, then glue to my ass. "Yogurt is fine if you have any," I said. "Or cold cereal."

"Unfortunately, I don't have any yogurt or cereal. You're stuck with pancakes or waffles." He sipped his mug as he waited for my reply.

Another glug of coffee to fortify myself wouldn't hurt. "It's fine, I usually don't eat breakfast."

"A little meat on your bones wouldn't hurt at all." Damien's blue eyes weren't cold as they met mine, instead, they had a rare gleam of humor in them. Something I'd never seen at work.

My cheeks flushed with color. "Fine." I took a seat at the counter. The pancakes did look delicious, at least. At this rate, they'd have to roll me out the door if the storm lasted.

Damien's fluid and precise movements held my attention as he flipped the pancakes and tended to the bacon. His short black hair still shone damp from the shower. I stole glances at his well-toned arms, and an image of him in the shower flickered through my mind in vivid color. Damn it.

"Katie." Damien caught my gaze as though he'd heard my wandering thoughts. He set a plate in front of me. "Breakfast is ready."

"Er, thanks." The pancakes were light and fluffy, flavored with vanilla, with butter and syrup on top. The food tried to catch my full attention, but I couldn't stop my hyper-awareness of Damien. The way his strong hands held the fork, the muscles in his forearms flexing with each movement, the way his lips wrapped around the bacon strip before biting it off.

I fixed my attention back on my plate. Its contents were safe to look at.

My phone pinged and I checked my texts.

It was from Connor, my neighbor.

> Just FYI. Max is having a flare up.
> When are you due back?

Worry clenched my stomach, and I set my fork down to reply.

> No flights out of Aspen right now.
> Weather says another day until the
> storm passes. Do I need to try to
> drive? It's 30 hours, waiting for a
> flight might be faster.

> He should be ok. I'll ping if
> anything happens.

I thanked him then tapped my fingers on the table, frowning.

"Iis something wrong?" Damien asked.

I glanced up at him. He watched me, a slight frown on his lips. Was he worried about me? Nah, probably not. "Nothing terrible." I forced a smile. "My brother's having some symptoms, but it should be okay."

"Ah." He took another bite of his pancake.

Wanting Damien was dangerous. This was just another day, just a meal shared between a boss and his assistant.

As though it heard me lying to myself, my heart raced when our gazes met, the intensity making my hormones sit up and beg.

I needed to get a grip. My mind had wandered into dangerous territory.

Business conversation should help. Or maybe suggesting we decorate to pass the time. He'd be snapping in no time, and everything would be back to normal. Though I did need to make sure Damien knew my priority.

"If something goes wrong with Max there's a way out of here, right? If I need to leave quickly?" I asked.

He paused, considering the question. "It depends. What's the issue with your brother? You've never said what his health problem is."

My muscles tensed and I hesitated before answering. "He's got an autoimmune disorder," I said quietly, staring down at my food like it held the answers to all my problems.

"I'm not familiar. Is it something that can be cured?" Damien asked, unusually gently.

"We both wish. With treatment, Max should be okay, but it's expensive and a flare-up can make him sick pretty quickly." I swallowed hard. "It's been a constant worry for me ever since our mom left."

"Your mother left you?"

I shrugged. It was an old wound, not so tender anymore. "She had better things to do with her life than take care of a sick kid. She would've taken Max with her if she *had* to, but she made it clear she didn't *want* to. We haven't spoken in years."

"Family's all we've got in the end, really," Damien said softly. Something about the way he spoke and the light in his eyes made me look at him twice. It was strange to see the billionaire mafioso looking at me with such understanding, and it only made me more nervous.

"Yeah. Yeah, it is," I said. For a moment, we simply stared at each other, our shared pain and vulnerability resting between us like a tangible force.

"Let me know if anything happens." Damien went back to his breakfast, but the firm note in his tone made my chest tighten.

I didn't say anything but fiddled with the pancake, my appetite gone.

"Do you have any siblings, Damien?" I asked, then winced. "I'm sorry, I don't mean to pry."

Damien gestured with his hand as if to brush my embarrassment away. "I had a younger brother once. His name was Antonio. He died very young. Our parents were killed by the same car bomb."

"Oh, no," I said, shocked by his revelation. It was hard to imagine the ruthless man in front of me experiencing such a profound loss. "I'm so sorry."

"Life in the business is not without its dangers," he said. "After the attack, I struck out on my own. I kept in touch, of course, but I wanted to make my own way." He smiled. A cousin of my age has twin daughters a little younger than you."

The weight of his memories pressed down in the air. "So do you still work with, uh, your original family, or did you find your own?" I asked, unable to contain my curiosity.

"My mother was a Santini." He looked away to stare out the window at the snowflakes drifting through the air. "A good portion of my business is outside *the* business so that we have a toehold in the legal world. I plan to have a family of my own. I created something that is mine, so perhaps my sons will be able to follow a different path if they wish." He ducked his head and grinned at me. "I'll admit my mother's sister has women lined up whenever I go to visit."

I choked on my coffee at the mental image of a cattle call to marry Damien.

"Look at the time," he said smoothly, setting his fork down. The moment of vulnerability vanished as though it had never existed. Yet something had shifted between us, a subtle change that left me both exhilarated and nervous in equal measure. Maybe just a bit more nervous.

"If you'd double-check the numbers on the Brindosin project?" It wasn't a question despite the inflection in his tone.

I nodded and headed upstairs to my laptop.

Then I paused and said over my shoulder, "I *am* on vacation, Damien."

"Katie." His words were pure seduction, low and sultry.

Turning on the stairs, my gaze locked with his. The spark of attraction flared between us, an unspoken desire that needed to stay unspoken. It would be so easy to give in, to let myself be swept away.

Then be sad and possibly without a job afterward. Or dead. Stupid idea, horrible. No, thanks.

"Yes?"

"Don't hide in your room. Stay down here."

After one nod, I jogged up the stairs, grabbed my laptop from my carry-on and stared out the window for a moment. The storm outside raged on, snowflakes swirling past the window like dancers at a wild party.

The memory of his words put a block of ice in my gut, reminding me of just how perilous this newfound connection could be. Even so, I couldn't deny that part of me longed to explore it further, to find out just how deep the rabbit hole went between us.

I wouldn't allow myself to be swept away by Damien's dangerous allure. Even as I made that vow, I damn well knew resisting the pull between us might be beyond me. Especially if Damien elected to act on the attraction.

He was sitting on the couch staring out the window when I came downstairs, and a brilliant idea sprang to mind. Why not ask him about decorating? He used this place for gatherings. There had to be decoration somewhere in it.

"Here I am, and I have a great idea. Instead of working on the contract, why don't we decorate here for Christmas? You have decorations, don't you?"

His brows rose and his expression shifted to the sardonic. "I do. I take it there will be no peace unless there is tinsel in sight?"

I curved my mouth into a triumphant smile. "Correct."

Damien shook his head and said, "This way." He headed up the grand staircase, and I hurried to catch up with him.

Halfway up, my foot caught, and I stumbled.

Damien steadied me, his hand resting firmly on my arm, and then he moved around behind me to place his hand on my lower back. His warmth spread through the silk of my blouse, and I fought the urge to lean into his touch. "Are you okay?" the damnable man asked softly.

"Of course. I'm not usually very clumsy, I just caught my foot."

"I know you aren't." He gestured for me to walk ahead of him.

At the end of the hall on the second floor, he opened a heavy wooden door and flipped on the lights. "After you."

I gasped. Rows of shelves lined three of the walls, each neatly labeled with a season and filled with identical plastic totes. On the fourth wall, an entire table was covered in rows of gift bags, sorted by color, tissue paper peeking out the top.

"What is all of this?" I said, unable to hide my surprise.

Damien shrugged, hand brushing my arm to direct my attention to the shelves. "Emergency presents. In case I ever go completely insane and have unexpected visitors over the holidays."

I snorted, shaking my head. Trust Damien Santini to be prepared for any scenario, even spontaneous Yule-tide cheer.

"Well, since you're so eager to celebrate." He waved a hand at the boxes. "Pick your poison."

My eyes lit up. I hurried over to the winter shelves and pulled a tote out and set it on the floor, pulling the lid off. It was full of neatly coiled LED lights. The familiar plastic-y aroma of them made me smile. The next tote rattled gently, full glass ornaments in all the colors of the rainbow, still in their boxes. Opening another, tinsel garlands in silver and gold and red, oh my, crackled under my fingers.

A ginormous tote held a disassembled tree.

Damien leaned against the door, watching me. "Is this enough of a fix, or do we need to put them up?"

"Definitely need to put them up. Help me carry them downstairs." I was halfway down the staircase when it dawned on me that I'd ordered him around. Oh, crap. At least he hadn't gotten angry.

It took three trips to get everything downstairs. I pulled up a playlist of Christmas music on my phone and cheerful sounds filled the air.

Damien's expression of long-suffering intensified, and I choked back laughter.

"Could you assemble the tree while I start putting up some lights?" I opened the light tote with a contented grin.

"Is there nothing that will convince you to cease this insanity? A raise, a vacation to an exotic island?" he rumbled.

I hesitated at the thought of a raise, but he was just joking. "Nothing, You can invite people over for Christmas, and it would surprise them so much."

Within minutes, I'd strung soft white lights around the living room. The tree turned out to be on the small side and only took a short time for Damien to set up.

Damien came up behind me as I clipped the final light to cleverly hidden hooks on the walls, close enough that his breath stirred the hair at the nape of my neck. "Not bad for a madwoman."

I laughed, turning to face him. "Speak for yourself, I happen to love Christmas."

One corner of his mouth quirked up. I was momentarily stunned by the transformation of his usual scowl into an actual smile. My stomach did a slow roll as I stared up into those icy blue eyes.

"Is that so?" he tilted my chin up with one finger. I licked my lips as his gaze darkened. "Then I suppose a little holiday cheer might not be so bad after all."

"Time to decorate the tree," I squeaked.

His brow raised, still gazing at my lips. Then his phone buzzed, saving me from melting into a Frosty-the-Snowman-sized puddle.

"I have to take this. Stay here. I'll be right back."

He strode from the room before I could respond. It was a sight worth ogling. Damien was very well built, and as far as I knew he didn't have eyes in the back of his head, so enjoying it was a treat without risk.

I released a breath, my heart racing like I'd just run a sprint. What was I doing? This was Damien Santini, for God's sake, not to mention the fact that he was nearly twice my age and involved in some very dangerous business. Making him think I was interested in him would be nothing short of disastrous.

I shook my head and busied myself putting ornaments on the tree. As much as I tried to talk sense into myself, I couldn't ignore the flutter of excitement in my belly at his nearness or the heat in his gaze. Smart me had decided to take a Christmas break. At least one of us got a vacation.

Moments later, the lights flickered and then went out. The room was now awash in the soft glow of twinkling battery-powered LED Christmas lights and tinsel. I sagged against the couch, my pulse racing as I took in the unexpectedly romantic scene.

Pretty, but the power out in the middle of a snowstorm was not a wonderful life.

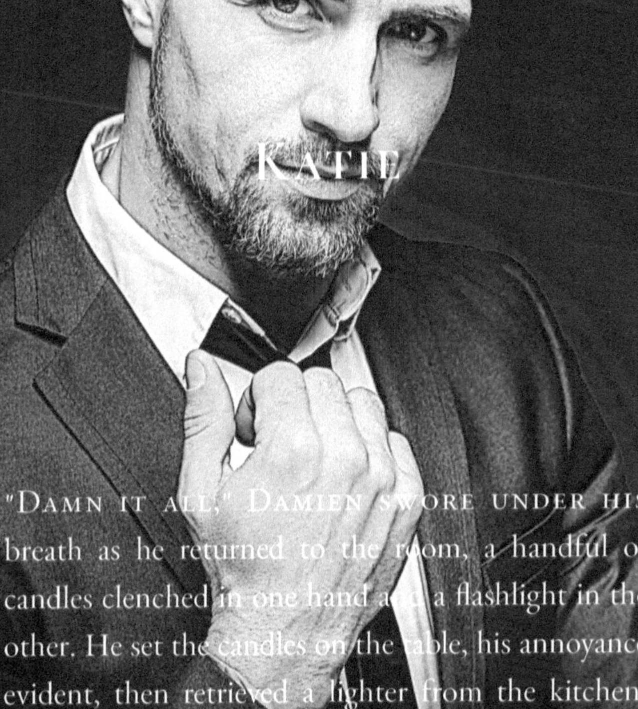

Katie

"Damn it all," Damien swore under his breath as he returned to the room, a handful of candles clenched in one hand and a flashlight in the other. He set the candles on the table, his annoyance evident, then retrieved a lighter from the kitchen. "Power's out, which means the blasted internet is too. The generator hasn't kicked on. I'm going to go out and check it. Get these lit."

Yes, sir. I nearly saluted him but bit back my irritation and lit one before searching for a plate to stick them to. Damien hadn't included any candlesticks. Come to think of it, why didn't he have any LED candles... Flashlights?

Ten minutes later, by the time His Majesty returned, snow melting in his hair, they were all lit, casting flickering shadows around the cabin. I'd stuck them to several small plates using wax drippings. "Generator's not working either," he said in a growl.

Without waiting for me to give an opinion, Damien exited again and returned carrying several logs from what I assumed was a storage or a garage.

"Do you need any help?" I asked. "Does this happen often?"

"No." His answer was curt. "Yes. Kind of. It happens just often enough that I keep supplies here. Normally it doesn't last long, but with the current weather and a guest, I'm not going to take any chances."

He carefully arranged the wood, his large hands stacking each log with precision. He sprinkled what looked like cut-up paper beneath the logs and lit the small heap. Flames shot up, and the logs ignited.

With warmth assured, I walked over to the window, peering out into the snowstorm that raged outside. The world beyond was relentless, thick snowflakes falling at an alarming pace, obscuring our view, and making it near-impossible to see anything beyond the veil of white. My stomach tightened with worry. we were truly trapped here now, at least for the time being. I hoped Max was okay, but I'd gotten no texts. No news was good news.

Now what? "Hey, do you know if there are any board games around?" I asked, trying to inject some positivity into the situation. "We should probably preserve the charge on our laptops and phones, just in case."

Damien grumbled something under his breath about poor maintenance. I hoped that didn't mean whoever was in charge of the generator wasn't going to get a visit in the middle of the night once this was over.

I gave Damien a small smile and raised my brows.

He nodded toward a corner cabinet.

I should've known he'd have a selection. I crossed the room and opened the cabinet. The assortment of firearms on the middle shelf caught me a little off guard. This was the sort of thing I should be used to seeing but it always jarred me. Oh, the top shelf held an assortment of game boxes. Guns and games. Sure.

I pulled them out and made my way back to the table, setting them down.

"Might want to shut the cabinet back up," Damien said commandingly, leaning against the wall next to the fireplace.

Again, my hand wanted to lift into a salute. Yes sir, Mr. Santini sir. Ten-hut.

Keeping those thoughts safely *internal,* I went back to the cabinet and closed it. "I found Monopoly, Scrabble, and a chess set."

He grunted in response.

"Something to do later?" We were gonna get bored. The power wasn't coming on anytime soon. "Candlelight can be quite cozy, right?"

Damien scoffed, clearly unimpressed by my attempt at small talk.

Undeterred, I continued, "You know, they say that during times like these, people used to tell stories around the fire to pass the time."

He gave me a very level look. "Most of my stories would probably give you nightmares."

Someone was in full grumpy mode again. I opted not to answer and glanced down at my phone, putting it in power save mode, just in case. It was a little after one in the afternoon. Amazing how dark it could get during a blizzard, even in the middle of the day.

"Speaking of fire." I turned toward the kitchen. "It's my turn to cook. You can relax while I whip up something for us to eat."

"Fine," he muttered, sinking into a plush armchair near the fire. He watched me move about the kitchen, his gaze never straying too far from my movements. Every time I glanced his way, he was staring. It was hard to concentrate on food when he looked at me like that, like he was putting me on his mental menu.

Luckily, bread, cheese, and butter would make grilled cheese, and there was some canned tomato soup in the pantry. Which was good because grilled cheese was about the limit of my cooking skills. I lived on frozen food and sometimes takeout now that we had a little more money.

His freezer and fridge were full of what looked like nutritious food, but I had no idea how to cook it.

Thankfully, he had a gas stove, much like the balky one in my apartment, albeit way newer. The spark on mine didn't work half the time, so I was used to using a lighter to get it going. I had it fired up in record time and glowed a bit at the demonstration of competence in front of him. I, too, could fend for myself.

"Hey, look on the bright side," I said cheerfully, assembling the sandwiches. "At least we're snowed in with plenty of food, right?"

"Thrilling," Damien deadpanned, but there was the faintest hint of an amused spark in his eyes.

"Come on, Mr. Santini." I flashed him a warm smile as I spread butter on the bread and put the pan on the burner. "It could be worse. We could be stuck out there in the storm, freezing our butts off."

"True, I guess," he said, his scowl softening ever so slightly. "But I still don't like being cheated. I paid for the generator to be serviced and functional."

"Sometimes you just have to roll with it," I said. He snorted but relaxed into the chair. "Think of it as a short break. This won't go on for long."

"Maybe you're right," he said, and for a moment, the tension between us eased. The crackling fire, combined with the flickering candlelight and my attempts at cheer, slowly chipped away at Damien's anger. Definitely a good thing. People died when Damien got really angry.

I set the water on to boil and brewed tea as I warmed the soup and flipped the sandwiches. The enticing scent of melted cheese competed with the rich aroma of freshly brewed tea in the air.

"Smells good," Damien said, his voice still gruff, but slightly softer than before.

"Thanks." I plated the food as I tried to quell my nerves. Being around Damien made me nervous in the office in broad daylight. My knees wanted to quake right now. "Come to the table, it's almost ready."

Damien eyed the food warily before picking up the sandwich and taking a tentative bite. As the flavors exploded in his mouth–the tangy cheese, sweet tomato-ey soup, his grumpy demeanor started to crack. He chewed thoughtfully for a moment, then looked up with a hint of amusement.

"Damn, Katie, this is good," he said, his tone begrudgingly impressed. "I've never had this. Not a traditional food in my parents' house."

"Thank you." Sweet relief. Damien not hangry was a good thing.

As we ate, the warm firelight and flickering candlelight cast dancing shadows across Damien's face, softening his features. The sight made my heart race, but I forced myself to stop noticing those sorts of things, focusing instead on our conversation.

Easier said than done.

"Did you ever think you'd end up snowed in with me?" I smiled at Damien as brightly as I could, hoping he'd perk up even more. This was already about as cheerful as I'd ever seen him.

"Can't say I did." He picked up the other slice of his sandwich. "But I've had worse company."

"I'll take that as a compliment." I bit into my sandwich and nodded decidedly.

"Take it as you will." He arched one eyebrow. "A quick question. Does your mother still use your surname?"

Danger! Danger! All my instincts shrieked at once. Why did he want to know that? What was he thinking?

"I have no idea," I said carefully, scrambling to choose my words. "Though, it would make me unhappy if anything happened to her, even if we're not close."

He considered me a moment, then nodded.

Holy freaking crap. I looked down and ate my food, no longer trying to force a conversation.

After clearing up, the board games remained stacked on the corner of the table. Heaven preserve me from Damien trying to help my family relationships.

After half an hour of staring at the fire, I let my boredom guide my senses. "Did you want to play a game to pass the time?" I glanced over at Damien.

"Board games?" He snorted. "Do I look like the kind of man who plays board games?"

"Then why do you have them here?" I raised my brows in a challenge.

"Guests." He raised an eyebrow back. "But *I* don't enjoy them."

I stared at the boxes and tried one last time. "There's a chess set, too."

"Are you any good at chess?" he asked, his voice low and measured.

"I know the rules. " I offered him a bright smile as I pulled the case out of the stack.

"One game," he said. "When I beat you, we'll find something...*else* to do."

Looking down, I kept my expression prim. Damien was in for a bit of a surprise.

As I set up the chessboard, my mood lightened as happy memories rose of Max, my younger brother. We'd spend hours playing chess together. It was our little ritual, and over time, I had become quite good at the game. I never imagined that one day I'd be playing against a man who won at any cost—and some of the games he played involved lives.

For just a moment I wondered if I should throw the game.

"Are you ready?" Damien snapped me back to reality. Yes, I'd throw the game. That was the smartest thing to do.

"Of course." It wasn't like anyone was around to watch me beat him. Except me. I didn't matter. Throw the dang game.

The chessboard lay between us on the polished wooden table, an exquisite work of art with elaborate carvings around its edges. The rich mahogany wood contrasted beautifully with the ivory and ebony pieces that stood like miniature soldiers, poised for battle. It was a gorgeous set.

I glanced at my boss across the board, taking in his imposing figure. He'd leaned back in his chair, his dark blue shirt and the candlelight accentuated his broad shoulders and strong jawline. His piercing blue eyes locked onto mine.

"Your move." He sounded like he already knew the outcome of this game.

I inhaled the scent of cheese and firewood that lingered in the air and selected a pawn. The familiar feel of cold marble beneath my fingertips reminded me that I was good at this. Like *good*-good. I could beat him.

Who was I kidding? No way I could throw this game. I moved my pawn two spaces forward in a classic fool's mate opening.

"Interesting choice." Damien narrowed his eyes slightly as he considered his response, then gracefully picked up a knight, hand moving with calculated precision. Had he thought I'd moved randomly, or did he know I was trying to trap him?

"You sure that's your move?" I leaned forward, my emotions a jumble. What if I pushed him too far? What would the consequences be? My competitive streak wouldn't stand down, which also made my fear spike.

"Careful." He looked at me over the board. "Consider what we might do for the rest of the afternoon, once this game is over."

His words sent goosebumps all over me, intensifying the electric atmosphere between us.

"Maybe I'll win." I grinned. There was something exhilarating about challenging him this way, even if only through a game of chess.

As the game progressed, my determination never wavered.

It took a few minutes, but I took advantage of Damien's first careless move, forcing him onto the defensive. My heart raced with every captured piece, the thrill of potential victory fighting the tension of playing against someone as dangerous as Damien Santini.

After I captured his knight, his initial overconfidence faded, replaced by a more serious demeanor as he figured out he was dealing with a real opponent.

"Feeling pressed?" I asked, innocence oozing from every pore, eyes big and eyebrows raised. I bit my lip to stop the smile when his jaw clenched just slightly.

"Pressed?" He scoffed, his gaze on my mouth. "You've merely caught my attention."

I lowered my lashes and examined the board.

When I moved my knight, Damien drummed his fingers on the table beside the board, considering his options. Watching him figure out that he might not walk away from this game as the victor filled me with an obscene amount of satisfaction.

"You're an aggressive player," he said, but he didn't seem put out. His tone was closer to a purr than anger. Oh, my.

"Yes," I said. "Aggression has its place—in chess."

"Very well," he said, finally making his move. His fingers brushed mine as he captured one of my pawns. The heat of his touch ran straight from my hand to my core. I fought the urge to pull back, not wanting to show any weakness in front of him.

"Your move." Damien stared at me, not the board.

I met his gaze, determined not to let him see how much he affected me.

Mistake. The look in his eyes ignited all my hormones in a bonfire. It took a moment to catch my breath.

"All right." I moved my bishop and threatened his remaining knight. "Your turn."

Our game continued, electricity dancing in every touch, every glance, every word spoken between us. Something forbidden and irresistible beckoned me. But I couldn't afford to lose myself in those sensations. I needed to stay focused if I wanted to win.

"Is it too late to ask for a five-minute break?" I asked, feigning innocence as I looked up at Damien. He considered me over steepled fingers.

"Five minutes would hardly make a difference," he said. "I suggest you focus on your next move."

"Of course, Mr. Santini," I said sweetly, lifting my hand and moving my queen without breaking eye contact. Holy crap I'd been cool as a cucumber.

He shifted his gaze from me to the board and rolled up his sleeves. He frowned at the board as he revealed sinewy muscled forearms.

My mind went straight to a vivid image of him showering. Or stretched out in the firelight. Damn it.

"Interesting move," he said, his lips curling into a tight smile. I giggled at the sight—his smile looked more like a grimace than anything else. It helped to break the erotic tension in me as well.

"Thank you." I masked my amusement with a polite smile. "I do try my best."

"Clearly," he said. The intensity of his stare when he looked up from the board nearly sent me straight into the erotic tailspin again, but I held firm, refusing to break eye contact. He was testing me, trying to gauge my reaction, but I wouldn't give him the satisfaction of looking away.

"Your move," I nodded toward the board, gaze unbroken.

Damien leaned back in his chair, eyes calculating as he weighed his options, looking for a way to win.

"Very well," he said finally, setting up to try to take my queen.

"Is that all you've got?" I said, trying to keep the mood light despite the tension in the room.

He shot me a warning glance, but the corners of his mouth twitched upward ever so slightly. Even the great Damien Santini couldn't resist a little banter during a heated match.

"You wouldn't want to poke the bear, would you?"

"Of course not." I feigned innocence once more as I moved my queen out of danger. "I'm merely trying to keep things interesting."

"Interesting indeed," he muttered, turning his attention back to the board. His gaze flicked between the pieces, searching for an opening, any weakness he could exploit. It was fascinating to watch him in action, the way his mind worked like a finely tuned machine. It was impossible to ignore the raw power and magnetism radiating from Damien.

"Your move," he said, a wicked smile playing on his lips as he took one of my bishops.

After consideration, I slid my rook into position with a confident smile. Surprise filled Damien's eyes as I countered his long-term strategy, maintaining my lead in the game.

"Didn't expect that, did you?" I asked, trying to sound innocent but unable to hide the hint of mischief in my tone.

"Perhaps not," he said grudgingly, his fingers drumming on the table as he studied the board intently. The sound was rhythmic and hypnotic, making me more aware of my heartbeat.

He finally moved his knight, trying to close in on my castle, but I had already anticipated his plan. I swiftly captured his piece, placing it beside the growing collection of his fallen soldiers on the side of the board.

The frustrated heat in his eyes made me pause. While it was nice to have the upper hand, especially against someone like Damien, this might be too much of a good thing.

"Indeed," he said. Two moves later the tension between us grew thicker, almost palpable.

"Check." I positioned my bishop to threaten his king. Holding my breath, I watched as realization dawned on Damien's face.

"Very clever." There was a glint of admiration in his eyes, but it only made him more determined to win. "Our game is not yet over."

"Of course not," I said breathily, catching the double meaning all too well. "But I've got you on the ropes now."

"Perhaps." His fingers hovered over the board as he contemplated his next move. When he finally moved his king out of check, I nearly squeaked in excitement as he fell into my trap.

I pushed my pawn forward, and Damien's eyes widened with surprise, and something else, a flicker of heat that made my heart flutter.

"Bold," he said, the ghost of a smile touching his lips, and for a moment, I caught a glimpse of a different man beneath the cold, ruthless exterior. Just as quickly, it vanished, replaced once more by the calculating expression of a predator sizing up its prey.

"You don't seem like the type to appreciate a timid

opponent." Hopefully, that would soothe his ire at being beaten.

"True enough." He moved his queen forward to take my pawn. "But sometimes, boldness has...consequences."

With trembling fingers, I reached out and moved my queen, placing her two squares away from his king. Any move he made to escape her was threatened. "Checkmate," I said, my voice barely audible but carrying the weight of victory within it.

Damien simply leaned back in his chair, regarding me with an intensity that made my blood run hot and cold all at once.

"Very impressive," he said at last, the words laced with both respect and something else, a dark, almost predatory hunger. "I underestimated you."

The silence that followed as I tried to find a response stretched on forever.

"Tell me." His voice was low, seductive, and *delicious.* "How did you get so good at chess?"

I swallowed hard, trying to find my voice amidst the whirlwind of emotions churning inside me. "My brother Max and I used to play when we were younger." I forced myself to meet his intense stare. "When he'd have a flare-up, chess was one of the few things we could do together. Turns out I'm good at it."

"Interesting," Damien barely blinked as he studied me. "You've got quite a talent for it. It's not every day that someone beats me." His words were tinged with admiration and something darker, more possessive like he was claiming some part of me as his own.

I shivered, but not with cold, unsure what to do. I had no experience with a man looking at me like that.

To try to lighten the mood, I glanced at my phone. "We were playing for hours, it's already supper time."

He eyed my lips. I had a pretty good idea of what he was thinking was edible at that moment.

I headed for the refrigerator, babbling as I went. "Sandwiches again?"

"Certainly. While you prepare them, I'll open a bottle of Cabernet Sauvignon that would be perfect for celebrating your victory."

"Um, sure," I said hesitantly.

Making the sandwiches took almost no time at all, and he opened the bottle to let it breathe.

"Sit," he said softly, gesturing toward the plush sofa as I carried the two plates back. I moved to the seat before the fire, my chest heaving as I watched him pour two glasses of wine. The deep red liquid shimmered in the dim light, reminding me of the metaphorical blood that had been spilled in our game.

"Here." He handed me a glass. "To your victory."

"Thank you." I raised the glass to my lips and took a tentative sip. The rich, bold flavor danced across my tongue, like a sultry tango between lovers. It was intoxicating, much like the man who now stood before me.

I wolfed down my sandwich, hungry despite the sensual tension in the air. Damien poured a second glass for us both as I set the plates to the side, now only crumbs on them.

"Shall we move on to a different game for the evening?" Damien asked as he took a seat beside me on the sofa. "Or would you prefer to bask in the glory of your victory a bit longer?"

"Another game?" I asked, trying to ignore the way my pulse quickened at his proximity. "What did you have in mind?"

"Truth or dare," he said simply, a wicked smile playing on his lips. "Unless you're too afraid, of course."

"Me? Afraid?" I scoffed, my bravado a weak attempt to conceal my growing nerves. "You're on."

"You first," Damien said, his voice low and velvety as he leaned in closer, close enough that I could feel the heat radiating off his body. "Truth or dare?"

"Truth," I said, my chest tightening with fear and not a small bit of excitement.

"Have you ever wanted someone so badly that it scared you?" he asked.

"Yes." A blush rose to my cheeks as I confessed. "But I'm not going to tell you who."

Like it wasn't obvious.

"Fair enough." He nodded, his gaze like a caress against my skin. "My turn, then. Dare me."

"Kiss me." I shocked myself with my words as they tumbled from my lips like a prayer.

For a moment, there was nothing but silence, the air between us heavy with unspoken longing and unanswered questions. Then, for the first time, Damien truly smiled.

The heat from the fireplace licking my skin was nothing compared to the intensity of Damien's gaze on me. His piercing blue eyes burned right through me, sending shivers everywhere. They weren't from the cold. They were from anticipation.

He leaned forward, tipping my chin up with gentle but firm fingers.

No backing out now.

Then his lips were on mine, warm and demanding, and I melted into the kiss. His tongue touched my lips, and I opened them, letting him in. A passionate, all-consuming connection rushed through me and seared itself onto my very soul. I grabbed the expensive fabric of his shirt and hung on as if my life depended on it.

His strong arm wrapped around my waist and pulled me against him. As our tongues danced together, I mimicked him. The taste and smell of him filled my senses, making it impossible to think about anything else but the man in front of me. My body ached with a desire I'd never known before, and it terrified me just as much as it thrilled me.

"*Mi angelo*," he said when he pulled back, his voice deep and smooth like aged whiskey.

Holy freaking hell that was so hot.

His fingers brushed against my cheek, the touch butterfly soft, sending a jolt of electricity down my back. My breath hitched. I couldn't deny the attraction I had for him, but at the same time, the situation terrified me.

Losing my virginity to a powerful and feared businessman, much less one involved in the Mafia, had never been a part of my career plan, but somehow, here I was. Possibly I should have experimented more with sex, but I'd never had time after Mother left when I was eighteen. I didn't have the emotional tools to be casual about this.

"Damien, I—" He cut me off with a gentle finger on my lips.

"Shh." He kissed my cheek and worked his way down to my jaw. "Let's just be in this moment together."

Oh, man. His touch was so good. I gave up on gathering my scattered thoughts when he nipped my earlobe. I stroked his shoulder and chest—*he* felt good too.

Turning my head, I lifted my lips so he kissed me again, with heat that belied all the ice I'd seen in him at work.

"Damien," I said against his lips, but he cut me off again by slipping his hand under my shirt and covering my breasts over my thin, lacy bra. He pulled back, brushing a stray lock of my hair back from my face. "Don't be nervous about your job."

He'd misunderstood my misgivings. I didn't know how to form the damn words to say, hey, dude, I'm a virgin! The words wouldn't come.

"I can't promise you anything beyond this moment. But I *can* promise that you'll enjoy it and I'll give you no cause to regret it later. Your job won't be in jeopardy no matter what happens tonight."

The heat in those blue eyes belied his words, even more intense than his voice. A storm of emotions raged inside me. I wanted him, there was no denying the attraction between us, but it went against how I'd lived all my life. My entire adulthood, I'd sought safety so I could protect myself and Max. Here I was, on the brink of surrendering myself to a man who scared and aroused me in equal measure.

I ducked my head into his chest, unable to find words.

Damien took my hand and guided it to the bulge in his pants, showing me the evidence of his arousal. "Can you not feel how much I want you?" he asked, sounding nearly choked up. "I've never wanted *anyone* as much as I want you right now."

"Really?" I said into his neck. Why did that make me want to puff up like a peacock? He wanted me more than a supermodel? He sounded sincere. Why would he lie?

"Really," he said. "You have no idea what you do to me, *mi angelo.*"

He kissed me again, this time with more intensity. Cool air brushed my skin, my shirt hanging open. When had he done that?

Shyly, slowly, I did the same with his, getting all the buttons undone and then running my fingers over hard muscles.

The orange-gold flames of the fire danced in the darkness, painting a glow on my pale skin. Electricity ran through me as Damien trailed his fingers along my spine and unhooked the straps of my black bra. His warm touch lingered as I slid my arms out of the straps, and the fabric fell to my feet.

"So pretty," he said as his fingers traced the curve of my breast before lightly flicking the tip of my hardened nipple. His tongue followed, exploring and teasing until I let out a gasp of pleasure.

He grazed his lips across my nipple, and it tightened in anticipation. A delighted sigh escaped me as he continued to kiss and nibble, making my skin crawl with pleasure. His strong hands firmly held my other breast, kneading it while his tongue lapped at the sensitive peak.

I was hungry for Damien, so hungry that the rush of arousal tingling through me was almost painful.

"Damien," I moaned, and when his eyes found mine, I saw the same desire burning in them.

"Lift," he said, his eyes dark with lust.

I did as he asked, lifting my hips from the bed so he could slide my jeans off. Then he removed my underwear as well. Now I was naked before him, the sweet ache between my legs growing more urgent with every breath. He kissed me again hungrily, then drew back.

He pressed his palm against my stomach. "So pretty," he said in a voice filled with need. "Beautiful." His hand skimmed down my body, settling just above the juncture of my thighs.

His fingers moved deeper, and his thumb brushed over my most sensitive spot. I gasped, my body shaking with pleasure. His lips moved down my neck, to the swell of my breasts, and then lower still.

A sudden wave of desire crashed over me as Damien kissed me, his hands slipping lower until his fingers expertly teased and tantalized my wetness. The pleasure was unbearable, a deluge of intensity that filled me with an uncontainable intensity. I couldn't control my body as it shuddered in response to the deft touch of his fingertips. I felt myself reaching for something I had never even dreamed of before, spinning towards an unstoppable climax that surged up from deep within me.

"Damien." I whimpered, his fingers flicking against my hardened bud driving me wild. "Please."

"Patience, *tesoro*," he said against my lips. "I'm going to take my time with you."

My body was on fire, every nerve ending singing with ecstasy as the orgasm hit me, shattering in a burst of white-hot pleasure. The world stopped for a moment, spiraling off into nothingness until I was utterly alone in my head. When he pulled his hand away, I nearly cried out.

Damien rose, yanked off the remains of his clothing, and pulled me into his lap. His hardness pressed against my damp curls, and he moaned into my mouth.

On my knees, facing him, his hardness rubbing against me, I nearly said it, the V word, but he spoke first.

"Good girl," he said, his hand sliding down my back to rest on my hips. "Now, I'm going to give you a little taste of what it means to submit to me. A combined reward and punishment for winning our chess game."

With that, his palm connected with my ass, the impact vibrating through it like a tuning fork. I gasped in surprise as shock rippled over my skin and heat surged beneath it. It wasn't unbearable—more like a sharp, thrilling sensation that sent goosebumps all over me. My initial shock quickly gave way to an unexpected surge of pleasure, and I found myself craving more.

"Did you like that?" he asked, his voice husky and low as he watched my mouth move wordlessly.

"Yes," I finally said in the smallest voice, shocked at my admission.

"Good." Another slap landed, this one slightly harder than the first. "Because there's much more where that came from."

With the third slap, something inside me awakened —a hunger, a need, that had lain dormant until now. With each slap, I craved more. Each stinging impact only served to heighten my arousal.

"Please." I whimpered, my voice barely audible above the crackling of the fire. "I need more."

"You want my cock inside you. You want me to fuck you hard?" He punctuated his words with another searing kiss, one that left me breathless and wanting.

The dirty words worked much like the spanking. Moisture pooled, and I was pretty sure some was starting to drop down my thigh.

Damien pulled a packet from the end table drawer and ripped the foil, sheathing himself quickly. Then his hands on my hips guided me onto his erection. He thrust and moaned, and I gasped. It hurt and yet felt good at the same time. He stretched me, filling me. I was so wet he had no trouble sliding inside.

Could he tell? Did he know?

"God, you're perfect. So tight." He growled, his breath hot against my lips as I straddled him. I didn't move, taking a moment to get used to him inside me.

He pushed up with his hips and I couldn't help a small wince of pain. This was nothing as bad as the romance novels made it seem to be, but there was some pain.

"What is it?" Damien froze and tilted my chin until I met his gaze. "What's wrong?"

"I tried to tell you, but I couldn't." My words caught in my throat as my cheeks burned with embarrassment."

His jaw fell as he realized. "No. You're a virgin?"

I nodded once, looking down again. I wasn't ashamed of it, just afraid he might not like that for some reason.

"Fuck, Katie." He froze, then carefully lifted on my hips, repositioning himself. He buried his face in my chest, and soon sucked my nipples again, distracting me from the slight pain between my legs. When he moved again, he guided my hips so I lifted with him. Slowly, he eased in and out, and the pain disappeared as pleasure took over.

Before long, I was moving with him, finding a rhythm that brought more and more pleasure. The sensation of him inside me was like nothing I'd ever felt before, a lightning bolt of pleasure that left me reeling. My fingernails dug into his shoulders as he moved faster, driving me to the brink of ecstasy.

I whimpered, my hips bucking against him as my climax approached, looming like a tidal wave on the horizon. "I'm so close."

"Let go for me," he said. He moaned into my breasts, suckling and kneading as he moved faster, and then, with one final thrust, my world shattered into a thousand pieces with an orgasm of such intensity that it left me breathless and trembling in its wake. Damien held me tightly, his strong arms supporting me as I rode out the waves of pleasure.

He pushed forward, his body like a wave rising and cresting, then groaned and ground into me, groaning deep in his throat. Then he shuddered hard. I kissed him, still floating in the sea of pleasure.

"Good girl," he praised, stroking my back. "That was incredible, Katie. You were so tight, and you came like a goddess. Beautiful."

He scooped me up and carried me to the blankets on the floor. Damien lay next to me, his body warm against mine. I curled into him, feeling safe despite who I was falling asleep next to.

His hand slowly stroked my hair as he spoke softly. "You did wonderfully. Sleep now, beautiful."

THE MORNING LIGHT FILTERED THROUGH MY eyelids. While I was warm, bundled in blankets, my nose was chilly. I forced one eyelid open. We'd slept near the fire, and it had gone to glowing red and yellow coals. The smell of fresh coffee and something sweet cooking caught my attention enough to open both eyes. I sat up and shivered in the chilly air. Damien was in the kitchen.

He glanced at me. "Hold on, stay in the blankets. There's still no power. I'll put a few more logs on."

Since I was naked and my clothes were nowhere nearby, I wrapped up, then shuffled to the couch and hopped onto it.

Last night's events played back in my mind. The game, the unexpected tenderness from Damien, and the way his touch had set my skin aflame.

Now he wore a simple black t-shirt that clung to his muscular frame, which made watching him put the logs on the fire a treat as well. The loose gray sweatpants were a treat, too. Why did men look so dang good in sweats? His hair was tousled. A huge change from the expensive suits he normally wore. But I'd never really been alone before with him either.

Once the fire was blazing, he settled next to me on the couch and kissed me thoroughly. "Want some coffee?"

I blinked in surprise. This was definitely not the gruff, imposing boss I was used to at work.

"Yes, please."

"I brought clothes down for you, but don't feel you have to put them on," he said, gesturing to the armchair holding a handful of clothing. He smiled cheekily. "I don't mind if you stay naked all day."

He walked back to the kitchen and poured me a cup of coffee. The rich, inviting scent drew my blanket-clad self to the table. I added cream and sugar, and took a sip, letting the warmth spread through my chest. I winced as I sat down again. Both my rear and other bits were rather sore.

"Here you go." He slid a plate of toast and eggs in front of me. Those piercing blue eyes held so much warmth. Was this a Damien-doppelgänger?

As I munched on my breakfast, I studied him. He moved with a quiet grace that I had never noticed before, and his gaze seemed tender whenever it landed on me. I'd woken up in some sort of parallel universe where Damien Santini, scary boss extraordinaire had been replaced by a kinder, caring man whose attention warmed me even in the frigid house.

I glanced out the window at the snow, then checked my phone. No texts, but...I'd have thought Connor would let me know Max was ok. It had only been a day, and Max's flare-ups weren't usually serious, but they did make it harder for him to get around. He'd be safe with Connor. There was nothing I could do right now and worrying helped nothing.

I didn't text Max during hospital stays if I could avoid it. He was a light sleeper, and he got angry with himself for being sick. My texting him made him feel guilty for something he couldn't control.

I wished he didn't feel that way, but I tried to respect it.

"Is something wrong?" Damien asked.

"Everything's fine." I shifted my weight to accommodate to minimize my uncomfortableness. "A little sore."

"Ah," he said, walking around the table and kissing me. "I can help with that."

He pulled the blanket open and gazed down at me, a possessive light in his eyes. "You are beautiful."

Holy crap. My nipples hardened, partly from cold and partly from the tingling in my body as I squirmed. My soreness was now a strange mix of pleasure and pain.

A small smile crept across his lips, making him look devilishly sexy. "Poor Katie," he said, his fingers tracing delicate patterns on my thigh.

He knelt in front of me, positioning himself between my legs as he pushed the blankets more out of the way. The cold air brushed against my skin, causing goosebumps to rise. My breath caught as I realized what he intended to do.

"Relax," he said, his breath hot against my sensitive flesh. His hands gripped my thighs, gently parting them wider as he pulled me forward. My face flushed with embarrassment, but I obeyed. I had no power in me not to.

As his tongue made contact with my nub, I gasped, the sensation both soothing and electrifying. His skilled mouth worked wonders, taking my attention from my aching body, licking and sucking in a rhythm that had me writhing and gasping. My mind went blank, filled only with pleasure.

"Damien." My fingers tangled in his dark hair.

He hummed in response, the vibrations sending shockwaves through me.

My hips bucked against his face, my body begging for release.

"Please," I begged throatily. My orgasm built, threatening to consume me whole.

Damien only intensified his efforts, his tongue delving deeper, his fingers gripping my thighs tighter.

Then, with a cry that echoed throughout the room, I shattered, my entire body shaking with the force of my climax.

Damien didn't relent, drawing out every last bit of pleasure from me until I was a trembling, breathless mess.

He worked his way back up to my mouth as I shivered.

"Teach me," I said, looking into his eyes. "I want to do that for you."

He raised an eyebrow. "Easily done, *mi angelo*. I am clean, so there's no need for protection."

He rose, the sweatpants sliding off at my tug and revealing his erection. I hadn't had a chance to take a good look at it last night. It was, from my limited experience, large, and definitely beautiful, part of him.

Pressure on my shoulders took me out of the chair and to my knees in front of him. I glanced up.

"Use your tongue first."

I did as he asked, tentatively tracing the head with my tongue. The taste of him was salty and musky, not at all unpleasant.

"Good girl." He growled, his hand stroking my hair.

Encouraged by his words, I grew bolder, swirling my tongue around him and taking him into my mouth.

His hips flexed, pushing him forward, and I jumped.

"Relax your throat," he said, his voice strained.

I focused on doing so, trying to take him deeper despite my inexperience. I gagged slightly, but Damien's hand was in my hair to guide me.

"Yes, *cara*, more," he said, his breathing growing heavier. I couldn't stop a thrill at the knowledge that I was affecting him like this. It was intoxicating, this newfound power I held.

As I continued to work my mouth and tongue over him, I could feel him getting closer to the edge. His grip on my hair tightened, and his hips began to thrust deeper into my mouth. I braced myself.

"Swallow, Katie," he said in a near yell.

As Damien spilled himself into my mouth, I did.

For a moment, we simply remained in position. Then as I looked up, he pulled me to my feet. When I looked into his eyes, I found something that went beyond mere lust or satisfaction. There was a fierce possessiveness. He pulled me close, wrapping me in his strong arms.

"A bit less sore?" he asked, teasing.

"I think so," I said.

The room had lightened, and snow had stopped falling at some point. A pang of guilt hit me. I was enjoying myself while Max was sick.

My phone pinged, so I pulled away.

"What's wrong, Katie?"

"Max, my brother. That might be about him," I said. "I need to check."

Pulling the robe back on, I grabbed my phone. Connor had texted. I had service again.

> Call me.

"Hey, Katie." Connor picked up, his calm voice filling me with worry. Connor was always calm when everything went to hell in a handbasket.

"Is Max okay?" I asked. "Sorry, I don't have a lot of charge and the power's out here."

"That sucks, I'm sorry. Max has been admitted for observation. He's having a rough time. When are you getting home? I take it the big storm stranded you in Colorado?"

"Yes. I hope I can leave soon, but it was snowing pretty hard." Oh, no. I was afraid of this. I hated that Connor had to take care of Max, but more that I wasn't there to be there for my brother myself.

"Is there another number I can reach in case your phone loses all charge?"

Damien, who'd been listening, tapped his phone and nodded. His battery was much better than mine. I sighed in relief and gave the number. I'd memorized it long ago.

"I'll be back as soon as possible. Is he awake?"

"I think he's asleep. He just settled in and he's tired. I'll let him know you called."

"Thank you, so much. I'll make it up to you."

"You don't have to do that. Just get home safe." He hung up.

Damien regarded me. For just a moment, I thought I detected a flicker of jealousy. "Who is Connor?"

"A friend. He moved in next door a few years ago and he and Max hit it off. He works from home, and I asked him to keep an eye on Max since I had to go on a business trip." Even trying to keep my voice level, a hint of dryness crept in on the last sentence. "Thank you for letting me give him your number too."

He cupped my chin with his hand. "If it helps ease your worries even a little, I'm willing to do whatever is needed."

My heart skipped a beat as I processed his words. Was he truly offering support, or was this manipulation? I searched his face for any hint of deception but found none. His expression was open, almost happy, so unlike the ruthless man I knew him to be.

"Can I trust you?" I whispered. It was a dangerous question, one I shouldn't have asked.

His expression softened, and he used his other hand to brush a stray lock of hair from my face. "In this, *cara*, yes." His fingers lingered against my cheek for a heartbeat longer than necessary. "I know my world is frightening to you, but I promise to protect you and your brother."

I found myself leaning into it ever so slightly. I was playing with fire, but for the first time, I didn't want to pull away. There was something magnetic about this man, something that drew me in despite my every instinct screaming for me to run when my brain engaged.

"Damien." Our eyes remained locked. We were teetering on the edge of something, but I wasn't sure what. There was so much more to Damien Santini than met the eye, and I was suddenly desperate to keep the man under the ice.

I shivered, the cold air intruding, and smiled at him. "I need to get dressed."

His expression wolfish, he said, "Not on my account, *cara*."

"*Freezing*. I'm freezing." I headed to the chair where the clothes were piled and hurried into them. No underwear, which was a new thing for me. As soon as I was clothed, I moved as close as I could to the fire.

He laughed. "I can warm you up again."

He'd put the sweatpants back on and moved to the window, looking out at the pristine snow lying in drifts. The driveway was completely covered. There was no way to drive out of here at the moment.

Seize the moment, Katie. Make memories.

"Do you want to play in the snow?" I asked.

He turned to face me with a wide, incredulous expression. "Certainly, *cara*. There are abandoned coats and gloves in the closet. Try some on while I get my own. There's another storm coming later this evening, so this is a good time."

Frowning, I asked, "Is there any way to get to town? If there's another storm that's going to keep me here longer, I really need to leave first."

"I'm sorry, but the roads are covered and unplowed," he said.

A guilty part of me was happy we had a little more time away from the real world. That didn't stop the guilt, however.

I ran to the closet and rummaged, my fingers brushing against various coats before finally finding the kind I was searching for. The thick, black fake fur coat with its matching gloves would be perfect for the frigid, windy weather outside. It wasn't below freezing, but it was cold enough that I wanted to be bundled up.

Boots, boots, I needed boots. I spotted a pair that looked close to my size and hesitated. Gorgeous knee-high leather, but the snow would probably do a number on them. I shrugged. Warm was good and I'd brush them off thoroughly.

"Ready?" Damien asked, his voice deep and commanding as always. I glanced at him, taking in his tall figure clad in a dark gray cashmere coat that only served to accentuate his powerful presence.

"Yep." I slipped on the gloves and stepped out into the snowy morning with him. A gust of wind whipped my hair around my face, causing me to quickly yank up the hood of my coat. The cool air bit at my cheeks, leaving a mild sting in its wake.

As we walked, I noticed how Damien was still wary even in this setting. His piercing blue eyes scanned our surroundings with calculating ruthlessness, then when he turned to me, they were filled with warmth.

Geez. I was captivated by this rare side of him.

"Are you going to stand there all day?" His amused

tone snapped me out of my reverie. I'd been staring at him.

"Sorry." Heat rose in my cheeks. "I was just, erm, admiring the view." The words slipped out before I had a chance to stop them. Eh, oh well.

Damien chuckled, the sound low and rich like dark chocolate. "The view *is* nice," he said, his gaze lingering on me for a moment before he turned his attention back to the surroundings.

A mischievous idea took hold of me, and I had to act on it. I bent down, my gloved hands scooping up a handful of snow and quickly molding it into a ball. With a gleeful grin, I hurled it at Damien, laughing as it hit him on the side of his face.

"Did you just—" His eyes widened in surprise, but before he could finish his sentence, I took off running, laughing breathlessly as my feet sank into the deep snow.

"Get back here!" he shouted, amusement evident as he gave chase. His boots crunched on the snow behind me, steadily getting closer. My heart raced with exhilaration, thrilled by this playfulness.

Unfortunately, the deep snow and my shorter legs conspired against me, leaving me winded and slowing down. Damien closed in, his long strides giving him an advantage. In one swift movement, he tackled me, sending both of us tumbling down into the soft blanket of white beneath us.

I shrieked, more from surprise than fear, as a shower of snow fell from the overhead pines, blanketing us both.

Damien laughed, the sound rich and genuine, and something in my chest tightened at the sight of him so unguarded and carefree.

"Gotcha," he said, his face inches from mine, his breath warm against my freezing skin. Without warning, he kissed me, his lips firm and insistent, staking his claim. The world faded away, leaving only the two of us and the electrifying connection between us.

As he pulled back, the lights inside the house flickered to life. A pang of sadness hit me. When life returned to normal, would we still be like this?

"Come on." Damien helped me to my feet. "Let's get inside before we freeze to death. We can put up more lights."

I nodded, my hand still tingling from the touch of his skin as we made our way back toward the house.

For a moment, I allowed myself to indulge in the fantasy that we were just two ordinary people enjoying a winter vacation together, without the complications and dangers of our true lives. Even as the thought crossed my mind, I rejected it. It could never be that simple. Not for a man like Damien Santini and a woman like me.

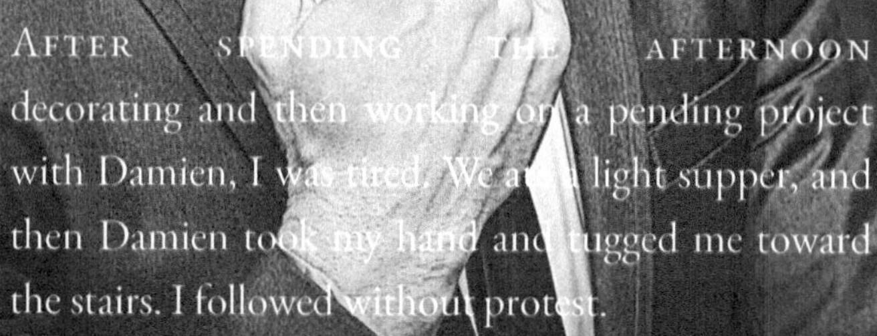

AFTER SPENDING THE AFTERNOON decorating and then working on a pending project with Damien, I was tired. We ate a light supper, and then Damien took my hand and tugged me toward the stairs. I followed without protest.

The gleam of snowflake-shaped Christmas lights we'd put in the hallway gilded Damien's face as he led me into his bedroom, shadows dancing across his sharp cheekbones and icy blue eyes. My heart thrummed with each step, anticipation, and nerves tangling in my stomach. It was hard to believe this was real.

He turned to face me, the hint of a smile tugging at the corner of his mouth as he slid his hands under my shirt, his fingertips grazing the sensitive skin of my waist. "It's my turn," he said in a low rumble. "And I'm going to take my time."

My core clenched at the dark promise in his words. I tilted my chin up, meeting his gaze with playful challenge. "You'll have to catch me first."

I darted away from him, stifling laughter as I ran to the other side of the massive bed. In a few quick strides he had me cornered, my back against the wall and his body pressed close. His scent enveloped me, sandalwood and something darker, more primal.

"Minx." He growled and captured my mouth in a searing kiss. Sparks ignited under my skin everywhere he touched, his hands roaming over my body as our tongues tangled. I moaned into his mouth, arching to get closer, needing more of his heat and touch.

He broke the kiss to lift my shirt over my head in one smooth motion, then his gaze raked over my exposed skin, like blue fire, and I shivered. "Perhaps you should wear less around me," he said.

"Hm. Could be possible now that the heat was back on." I grinned, teasing, but he didn't smile.

"I'd like that." He dipped his head to press a line of open-mouthed kisses down between my breasts as his clever fingers unhooked my bra.

The lace fell away, baring me to his view. He sucked in a sharp breath, fixated on my breasts. "Or nothing," he said hoarsely. "Take off the rest." The rough command sent a thrill through me, and I hesitated, uncertain. I'd never stripped for someone before.

He gripped my hair and tugged, pulling my head back so I looked up at him. "I won't ask again." His eyes were dark with lust.

Face flaming, I slid my trousers and panties down my legs.

Damien's gaze raked over me, lingering on my breasts and the apex of my thighs. "Yes. Naked when we are alone."

He shed his clothes with swift, economical movements, his body a work of art, honed by years of hard work. My breath caught at the sight of him, heat flooding my core.

Damien wrapped an arm around my waist and pulled me flush against him. "Like what you see?"

I blushed harder instead of answering.

"So sweet." He kissed and nipped his way down my throat, then palmed one breast, kneading and rolling my nipple between his fingers until it tightened under his touch. Pleasure sparked, racing down to pool between my legs. I whimpered, squirming against him, desperate for more.

A low chuckle rumbled in his chest. "Patience. We have all night."

He lowered his head to close his lips around my other nipple, laving and sucking until I thought I might come undone. Moans tumbled from my lips unbidden, my fingers clutching at his arms.

Damien released my nipple with a gentle scrape of teeth, shifting lower. He pressed a trail of open-mouthed kisses down my stomach, nipping and sucking at my skin.

"Please," I whimpered. I was so close already, strung tight as a bowstring. Knowing what to expect, what he could do, made it harder.

He nudged me backward, and we settled on the bed, which was good. My knees weren't working too well at holding me up right now.

"Not yet, *cara*." His breath ghosted over where I ached most, and I nearly sobbed. "You'll come when I allow it, and not a moment before."

He spread my thighs wider, settling between them. I gasped as his tongue glided through my folds, circling my nib but never quite touching. He gripped my hips, holding me in place against the mattress. I strained against his grip, desperate for more, but he was immovable.

Laughter rumbled against my core. "So impatient. Relax."

He slid two fingers inside me, crooking them to rub against that sensitive spot. My back arched off the bed with a cry. The coil of pleasure in my belly wound tighter and tighter, ready to snap.

I cried out again only for his fingers and mouth to disappear altogether. My eyes flew open as I whimpered in protest.

Damien loomed over me glaring at me. It wasn't anger. It was control. "Not yet," he said, wiping his slick fingers on my thigh. "You'll get your release when I'm buried inside you, *tesora*, and not a moment before."

He shifted, the broad head of his erection nudging at my entrance. I shuddered in anticipation, ready to beg if that's what it took. He only teased me, sliding through my folds and bumping my nub without pushing inside.

Laughter bubbled in my chest, edged with desperation. "You're a cruel man, Damien Santini."

His answering smile was wicked. "Cruelty can be pleasurable, in the right context." He rocked against me, dragging another moan from my lips. "Admit it. You like being at my mercy."

"Maybe." I gasped as he pressed into me slowly. So, so slowly.

"If you move before I permit it, there will be consequences." He thrust forward and I squeaked.

"You want me to just lie here?" The squeak as he thrust wasn't feigned. I didn't know if I could do it.

"For the moment. You move when I give you permission." He pulled out again, not quite filling me in the process. I really wanted him to fill me.

I gritted my teeth and tensed my muscles to keep from rocking against him. The gleam in his eye told me that whatever he had planned if I moved would involve even more torment.

The tension in me climbed higher and higher and I dug my nails into his shoulder.

"Little cat." He chuckled. "Move with me, *cara*."

I obliged gladly. My long-delayed orgasm ripped through me as we moved together. He didn't stop, and I peaked again, or maybe the first never stopped, as the hard fast thrusts brought him to climax with me. My cries echoed with his growl as I finished with him.

So much for all night. Sleep dropped over me like a brick, at least until Damien woke me to do it all over again.

Ah. So *that's* what he meant by all night.

DAMIEN

I enjoyed the warm weight of Katie curled against my side as she went to sleep. I ran a hand down the curve of her back, tracing the marks I'd left on her pale skin. Mine. Once her breathing was deep and even, I eased myself out of bed. There was much to do, and sleep could wait.

Pausing, I inhaled the scent of Katie and sex that still lingered in the air. An unaccustomed smile tugged at the corner of my mouth. I tucked the duvet over her, all lush curves and fiery hair. The urge to wake her to take her again stirred, and I tamped it down. Business first, third round later.

After a quick shower, I dressed and went downstairs to put out fires and light some of my own. I contacted my second-in-command, Rafe, ordering him to dig up what he could on this Connor, who lived next door to Katie, and any information on Katie's mother.

The background check when she'd been hired and then changed position would pop their names and at least some info. While no one had been flagged as a threat, I found myself keenly interested now.

I needed to find out if Connor was competition-in-waiting that needed to be snuffed out and what would be the best way to punish Katie's mother for abandonment.

While I waited for Rafe to report back, I sorted through the usual mess of issues that had piled up in my absence. Deadbeat clients late on payments, shipments gone awry, disputes that needed settling. Requests for funding, an investigation into a branch that hadn't been paying overtime correctly.

I made a note to slide that one to Katie to find out if the money had ended up in places where it shouldn't be.

I'd made a significant dent in the work when my phone buzzed. Rafe.

"Speak."

"Connor O'Hara lives next door to Ms. Jones, moved there about nine months ago. Running a deeper background check now. In the preliminary, he's a graphic artist and designer making a steady wage."

I tapped my fingers, filing the information away. Potential threat, but I'd wait for the full background check to come through before making any decisions. Raising the dead wasn't in my skill set if I acted in error.

"The woman?" I asked.

"Born Lindsay Holmstrom, aka Lindsay Jones, now Lindsay Deak. Age forty-six. No criminal record. She's married to a hedge fund manager named Ryan Deak. Living large in the Hamptons, from what I can tell."

My jaw clenched. The bitch had abandoned her children and now lived a life of luxury. Unacceptable.

What was the best way to strip her of everything? Decisions, decisions...

"Keep an eye on them," I said. "I'll decide how best to handle this situation once I've had time to consider."

I hung up and a yawn overtook me. It was time to return to the vixen in my bed.

Katie had kicked off the covers and then pulled them partially back onto her at some point. Naked, her hair a wild tangle of fire around her face, she looked well-fucked and utterly mine. A possessive warmth spread through me at the sight.

I stripped and pulled her into my arms, the scent of her soothing me into sleep.

I woke beside Damien in the pale light of dawn, chased out of sleep by an uneasy dream. Listening to his even breathing soothed my anxiety a little. His scent was subtle and intoxicating. But I couldn't get back to sleep, even though I was still tired.

Heat radiating from Damien's body, and I relaxed into it. He'd been warm and affectionate all yesterday. Even now, one of his arms was flung over me possessively.

Maybe a glass of water and checking my phone would help. I slipped from under his arm and pulled on a robe, moving silently to the door. He didn't stir, and I slipped out.

No more news from Connor, so I messaged him.

Is everything ok?

Waiting for his answer, I sipped water in the kitchen. Snow was falling again, tapping the windows gently.

Connor didn't answer. Since it was early, I waited to text again. I'd try in an hour and find out how Max's night had gone. Flare-ups tired Max out, so I didn't want to chance waking him up if he were resting.

Curiosity got the best of me now that the cabin was warm again. To pass the time, I explored the first floor of the expansive cabin, marveling at the opulence surrounding me.

In the study, floor-to-ceiling bookshelves lined the walls, filled with leather-bound volumes that gleamed in the light. I ran my fingers along their spines, tracing the delicate gold lettering, and wondered if Damien had read any of them.

He'd been a mystery to me outside of work, but now I wanted to know everything about him.

What should I do? Damien's life was dangerous, and I couldn't expose Max to that any more than I already had. There was a difference between working for Damien and sleeping with him. An enormous difference

Uncertainty and worry for Max gnawed at me as I continued exploring the cabin, unease nibbling at the back of my mind. I wandered to the back side of the cabin, where I'd never been. I assumed this was storage and garage since it's where Damien brought the wood from. There was a door at the very back.

I pushed the heavy door open, and the muted scent of gasoline and oil hit my nose. Flipping on the lights, an unexpected sight greeted me. A pristine garage with advanced, sleek snowmobiles that look like they'd been plucked straight from the pages of a luxury magazine parked on one side and an extensive woodpile on the other.

My eyes widened. We could have left at any time today. Or yesterday. He hadn't told me about them at all, robbing me of the choice to try to get to town and paved roads.

A rustle behind me made me jump. "Damien?"

He leaned against the doorway, his piercing blue eyes unreadable.

"Trouble sleeping?" His voice was still low and gravelly with sleep. He didn't sound mad, but it wasn't his place to be angry right now. It was mine.

"Why didn't you tell me about these?" I asked, gesturing toward the snowmobiles, my anger bubbling beneath the surface. "We could have used them to escape being snowed in."

"Escape?" He raised an eyebrow. "Is that what you want, *cara mia*? To run away from me?"

"Don't deflect," I said. "I don't understand why you didn't give me the option. What if Max gets worse?"

He stepped closer, face and voice colder than the ice outside. "What if I told you there was a reason for my silence? A reason that involved you? An opportunity for both of us?"

My breath caught in my throat. He'd deliberately neglected to tell me. Hidden the information, which was as bad as lying to me. The sting of betrayal burned through my chest, and I struggled to swallow the lump forming in my throat. "You wanted to keep me here just to sleep with me?"

He hesitated for a moment, his gaze searching mine before he finally nodded. "Yes, I did."

"Is that all this is to you? Some game where you use me for your pleasure?" Anger at myself for being so damn gullible stabbed through me, and I couldn't keep the fury out of my voice.

"Katie—" He reached out to touch my arm.

I recoiled. "I can't believe I was so stupid to think you cared about me. That I felt something for you."

My eyes burned, and I put everything I had into keeping the tears from falling. He would *not* see me cry over this.

Damien gripped my shoulders. "Listen to me,"

"Listen to what? There's nothing to talk about." I shoved at his chest. "I'm done, Damien. I'm not a plaything."

"Damn it, Katie, it's not like that." His voice became even cooler and more precise. "Yes, I wanted you. God knows I've never wanted anyone as much as I want you. But it's not just about sex."

"Really? Then what else is it about? Blow jobs?" I scoffed, glaring at him.

In one quick movement, he scooped me over his shoulder and headed back into the cabin.

"Let me down!" I yelled and snarled.

He swatted my behind as he strode into the living room and dropped me on the couch, pinning my arms. "Calm down."

"Let go of me!" This wasn't exactly the most stellar way to get me to stop struggling.

"Not until you listen." His face hardened as he adjusted his grip on my arms.

"To what? Excuses?"

"Do you think I've *ever* excused myself to anyone?" He stared down at me, expression dangerous.

Self-preservation belatedly reared its head. "Honesty and trust are important," I said in a small voice.

"So is this." His mouth crashed down on mine, angry and demanding.

Rage and desire warred within me as I bit down on his lip, hard enough to draw blood. He merely laughed, the sound dark and dangerous, sending a thrill up my back.

His hands were everywhere, grasping and squeezing roughly. My robe fell open, and I moaned into his mouth as his fingers found my nipples, pinching and twisting until I whimpered.

He broke the kiss, trailing his lips down my neck as he untied the sash of my robe. The fabric fell to either side of me, leaving me bare before his gaze.

"You're mine," he growled, securing my wrists above my head with the sash.

I strained against the bindings, panic, and desire mingling until I couldn't tell one from the other. My heart raced as Damien's hands skimmed down my sides. His touch was both tender and possessive, as though he couldn't decide whether to worship me or claim me.

Perhaps it was both.

He stripped, then positioned himself at my entrance. I tugged on the sash confining my wrists. I might have been able to get them free, but I wasn't entirely sure I wanted to. I wasn't entirely sure I didn't want to, either.

Our eyes locked, anger and lust swirling within those icy blue depths, as well as something else I couldn't identify. I glared up at him as I fought the ropes.

With a powerful thrust, he entered me. I cried out at the sudden intrusion, clenching around him.

He stilled, jaw clenched, eyes boring into mine. "Say it," he said. "Say you're mine."

I bared my teeth, refusing to give him the satisfaction. He pulled back until just the head of his cock remained inside me, the emptiness nearly unbearable.

"Say it," he said. "Or I'll leave you wanting."

The threat was clear. I squirmed, then decided to yield for the moment. I didn't have to mean it.

"I'm yours," I said. Despite not meaning them, when the words left my mouth, they felt real. Too real.

Triumph lit his expression as he slammed into me again. The pace he set was punishing, each thrust pushing me higher and higher until I shattered around him with a scream, wrapping my tied arms around his neck.

He followed soon after, burying his face in my hair with a groan. We remained there for a long moment, panting harshly as the anger seeped from our limbs, leaving only a sweet release in its wake.

Damien placed a gentle kiss on my cheek.

I turned my head away, staring at the far wall as he withdrew from my body. The evidence of our passion trickled down my thigh, a reminder of how deeply I'd gone into his web. Pregnancy had suddenly come onto the table. I wasn't on any form of birth control other than abstinence.

What should I do? Oh, damn it.

Damien untied my wrists, massaging the tender flesh there. I kept my eyes averted, unwilling to meet his gaze. What had I done? This wasn't me.

One moment we were fighting, anger hanging heavily between us, the next our mouths and bodies had collided in a clash of teeth and tongues and greedy hands.

Now...now I didn't know how to feel. My body still thrummed with pleasure, but my mind was in turmoil. I cared for Damien, far more than was wise, but being with him was like dancing with the devil—intoxicating and dangerous all at once.

"Look at me." His tone was soft but brooked no argument. I lifted my gaze to his, heart twisting at the warmth I found there. It made me want to believe he could be tender, that there was more to him than just ruthless ambition. Cold common sense told me not to hold my breath.

Damien cupped my cheek. "You're mine now, Katie. We were made for each other."

I knocked his hand away, scrambling off the couch to grab my robe. "I don't belong to you," I said, anger rising once more. "No one owns me."

"Keep telling yourself that." He stood as well, stalking toward me like a predator after its prey. "You can deny it all you want, but you know the truth. You admitted you're mine, not five minutes ago."

"Go to hell." I stood my ground, glaring up at his smug face. "I only said it to get my rocks off."

He grasped my chin, tilting my head back. "I've already been there, *cara*. Now come to bed."

I wrenched out of his grip, clutching my robe tight. "No."

For a moment I thought he might pick me up, but then he shrugged. "As you wish. This isn't over, Katie."

My chest squeezed at the promise in his words. No, it wasn't over. Not by a long shot.

His phone rang, jangling the stillness. Mixed anger and amusement filled me as he went to check it. At least it hadn't happened in the middle. I wasn't sure what he would have done.

This was the first time it had rung this whole time. Normally, at the office, he got calls all the time. Strange.

"Hello, Bria." He held the phone away from his ear.

Someone was screaming in pain on the other end, and a female voice shouted, "Can you hear me now?"

I flinched.

Damien stared at me, then strode into the library.

My heart squeezed. I wanted to stay, so much, but Max needed me too and I couldn't afford to become Damien's plaything. Even if I couldn't quit my job, I needed to keep my heart and soul, what made me myself, my own, and not his toy.

I ran up the stairs. I needed warm clothing. I was leaving, right now.

I grabbed the heaviest clothing I could find and rushed to the closet where the gloves, coat, and boots I wore earlier waited for me, threw them on, and then ran for the garage.

I'd been four-wheeling with Connor and Max a few times this summer when Max had a good few weeks. The snowmobiles had the same setup—turn the key, then a button to push to start it. I hit the switch to open the garage door, grabbed a helmet, and then climbed on the running machine. Thankfully, the snow hadn't piled in front of the garage door.

Guiding it to the road was hard, even steering carefully. It was so cold it wasn't even funny when the wind picked up as it moved. Shivering so hard it felt like I was going to tear muscles, I gave up only a little way down the road. This was not going to work, no matter how much I wanted to leave, I turned in a wide U, then yelped as I went too far, and the machine and I went over the edge of the road, tumbling into the ditch and deep, soft snow.

It pressed me down, and I shoved, but I didn't have any leverage to get it off me.

At a pushing, trying to shift it off me.

It wasn't budging. I was buried on the side of an unplowed road, in the snow.

When had I turned into such an idiot? Oh, yeah. About the time Damien Santini stuck his dick into me.

"Bria," I said into the phone, low and serious. "We both know information obtained under torture is often inaccurate. I'd suggest getting any names he might have from him immediately. If you can pause the session for a day or so, ask him again to confirm the details he's told you. Presumably, he knows he's going to die, so he has every incentive to make up stories to buy more time. So weigh what he tells you carefully."

I was restating what she already knew, confirming it so she could better leash her impatience.

A hint of pride warmed me as I leaned against the wall, my free hand running through my hair. She was good at information gathering. I'd have her in my organization in a heartbeat if it weren't for her loyalty to her sister, and by extension the rest of the Montrelli clan.

"Damien, what would I do without you?" she asked with a dry laugh that lightened my heart. "Father's forbidden your name being mentioned again. And thanks for the new phone. He's got my other one jammed full of spyware."

Ever since she was a child, I'd encouraged her ambition within the family, partly because I genuinely liked her, and partly to irritate her father, who I couldn't stand. Her twin, Carina, was a sweet girl, but uninterested in the family business.

"I cherish thwarting him, yes, but I have to go. I have a personal issue to deal with."

Bria chuckled. "Have fun. And thanks, I needed to get out of my head for a minute. I was getting too involved in the torture, I almost missed him admitting he was involved in Tony's killing."

She did rather enjoy inflicting extreme pain. She had a reputation for it among the other families and used it well.

Leaving the study, I stopped to listen for where Katie had gotten off to.

The cabin was silent. My gut clenched with an unfamiliar emotion—guilt.

A quick search didn't find Katie in the bedrooms or anywhere else. Snow peppered the windows as I headed for the garage, hoping she hadn't decided to try to move one of the snowmobiles. Frigid wind and snow in the garage. The door was open and one of the snowmobiles was missing. Panic gripped my chest like a vise. The roads around here could be tricky, especially for someone who wasn't an experienced rider.

"Damn it, Katie," I muttered, fear and frustration coursing through my veins. I strode to the equipment locker and grabbed my snowmobile suit, gloves, and boots. I pulled a second one for Katie. There was no telling what she'd cobbled together to wear.

My heart pounded with adrenaline as I hurried into the protective clothing, each second like an eternity.

She'd taken a helmet, but no other gear was gone. My worry deepened.

The snowmobile roared as I sped off toward the road in search of her. The helmet shielded my face from the cold wind, and I had to throttle back to make sure I didn't skid. Worry and regret flogged me as I squinted in the path of the lights, marking the tracks of her machine's tread.

The snowfall grew heavier. My grip tightened around the handles of the snowmobile as I checked Katie's location on my phone. If she found out I'd done that there'd be another fight, no doubt.

Her dot blinked on the screen on the road not too far away, not moving. In this worsening weather, it felt like miles away.

The damned snow was falling fast and thick. The second storm had moved in sooner than anticipated.

Headlights on, I moved forward slowly. The tracks were clear, though disappearing quickly, and I followed them. She'd made it down the road for a ways, then she tried to turn, and then the tracks went off the road. I stopped the snowmobile and ran to the edge of the road.

I leaned forward, staring down the slope. Katie was pinned under the snowmobile, pushed down deep in the snow,

"Please be okay," I prayed, my breath visible in the frigid air, as I started down into the ditch.

When I reached the machine, she stirred and looked up at me with scared eyes. She was pinned, but mostly because she had no leverage in her position. The snow showed she'd tried to push it up.

"Can you get out if I lift?"

Katie nodded, teeth chattering hard as she shivered. She wore the coat she'd worn when we played in the snow earlier and thin gloves. Worry about hypothermia suddenly leaped up the line of my worry.

She blinked her wide eyes at me. "I'm cold. I'm not a toy."

Her words were slurred. Fear clenched my heart in a fist.

"No, you aren't a toy." When I lifted the machine, she struggled to move, shivering hard. It took her a few tries, but she managed to crawl free of the damned machine.

Once she was out of the way, I dropped it and pulled the emergency pack out of the cubby. I unwrapped the emergency blanket and wrapped her in it.

She was moving well. That was a good sign. Getting her to warmth was my priority.

"I can't stay where I'm not valued." Again, her words were barely distinguishable.

"I know, Katie, *amore mio*. I'm sorry. I handled that so badly."

She staggered as I helped her to her feet. "Stay with me." I settled her helmet over her red-gold hair and pulled the face shield down. The next order of business was getting her into protective gear.

Once she was in the seat, I wrapped her in the emergency blanket and sat behind her. I tried to balance speed getting back to the house with chilling her further in the unrelenting wind and snow.

I parked in the front, right by the door, picked her up, and carried her into the house.

She stirred again, grumbling. "You don't listen."

"Correct, Katie," I pressed a kiss to her forehead. "I will in the future, I promise." Mostly.

I yanked her wet clothing off and wrapped her in blankets and towels, including her hair, leaving her near the fire as I brewed warm herbal tea.

After settling her on the couch, I disrobed and rewrapped the blankets around us both, giving her my body heat and holding the mug for her so she could sip easily. As her shivering slowly lessened over the cup of tea, I stayed by her side, beyond grateful for her safety and overcome with the intensity of my emotions.

When Katie was warm and had stopped trembling, she slept, her body pressed against mine.

A few moments later, her phone chimed.

The screen displayed an incoming message from her brother's number.

> I'm feeling a lot better. Back home now. Will you be home for Christmas?

Katie stirred and then nestled into my embrace. The scent of her shampoo filled my nostrils, and I breathed in deeply, committing it to memory as I tightened my hold on her.

I texted Alex with my instructions about what to do with her brother. As I did so, Katie stirred again in her sleep, her body seeking warmth and comfort from me. I set the phone down and held her tighter, allowing her to absorb every ounce of heat and protection I had to offer.

Watching her chest rise and fall with each breath she took, I marveled at how this woman had managed to burrow her way so deeply into my heart in just a few days, awakening feelings I'd never had to deal with before.

I didn't mind dealing with them now.

Oh, geez. It felt like someone had beaten me all over. Despite wanting to burrow deeper into the covers, I opened my eyes. I was on the couch with a blanket tucked carefully around me. The lights were dimmed, though I there was gentle tapping to my right. I slid my gaze in that direction, not wanting to move my head.

Damien sat in an armchair, using the end table as an improved desk, his laptop open. As if my open eyes were a signal, he looked up from his work.

This wasn't the first time I'd woken, but it was the first time I was up to walking or talking. Or moving at all. A more immediate need beckoned, though. I pushed at the covers.

"What do you need?" he asked, rising and steadying me as I swung my legs to sit up. "Can I help?"

"Bathroom," I said, strangely embarrassed. After all we'd done, I was still self-conscious about being in my underwear. Wait, I was wearing underwear? Someone must have done laundry. Surely not Damien. Ha.

With his help, I made the round trip safely, and once I was back on the couch, he offered me tablets and water.

"Painkillers," he said in answer to my questioning glance.

I downed them, hoping they would work fast. So many muscle aches. I was such an idiot.

Those piercing blue eyes studied me, searching for any signs of distress. "How are you feeling?"

"I'll live." I gingerly stretched, wincing at the ache in my neck and back.

Damien's hand settled on my shoulders, his touch light yet possessive. "You should eat. You've been sleeping for almost a day."

He spoke as though our quarrel hadn't happened, and it had. It had happened big time.

I shook my head, grimacing at the stab of pain the motion caused. "We need to talk. I need to dress."

"Katie." His tone held a note of warning, but I ignored it. I couldn't put this off any longer. I was so far out of my element that it was not even kind of funny.

Closing my eyes, I took a moment to compose myself. When I looked up, Damien was standing in front of me, a shirt in his hands. Before I could take it or react, he helped me into it. Oh, fine. I allowed it.

It was better to save my energy for the real issues, not this one. The consideration only made the ache in my chest worse. This ache no painkiller would touch.

While he'd saved my life, I couldn't forget he'd shown me that he didn't care about what was important to me. Knowing Damien, there would be no apology for what he had done.

I was tired, and sad, and just wanted this conversation over with.

When I was fully dressed, I lifted my chin and met his gaze. "Thank you for coming and getting me. You saved me, and I fully recognize how much of an idiot I was for leaving. That doesn't mean the other important things have changed. They haven't."

Damien stared at me for a long moment. I resisted the urge to fidget, keeping my stance firm.

Finally, he spoke. "We'll have this discussion after you've eaten and drunk, then. You expended a lot of energy."

The Christmas decorations made the room look so warm and inviting. I sighed. "Fine."

Damien brought me coffee and toast. The familiar aroma helped settle my nerves, at least.

After a few sips, I set down my mug and arched an eyebrow at Damien. He was watching me closely, that unreadable expression on his face. It was now or never.

"This can't work," I said quietly as I set the plate on the coffee table. My fingers twisted in my lap, nerves warring with determination. "I'm devoted to my brother. To Max. You ignored that. You manipulated me in a lot of ways, and I can't forget that either."

Damien's jaw tightened, but he remained silent. I rushed on before I lost my nerve, or he interrupted.

This was the scary part. "I'm afraid to even say this, I know how, um, how your *business* handles these things, but I can't work for you anymore, not after everything that's happened." I swallowed a gulp of coffee. "I hope you can understand and trust I will keep your business to myself."

The silence stretched. When I finally dared to peek up at Damien again, his eyes were shuttered. He'd turned cold.

I sat very still, half-expecting an explosion of anger, but he only regarded me in silence. The moment lasted forever, seconds ticking into minutes until I started to squirm in my seat.

Damien rose, stepped to my side, and knelt beside my chair, head bowed. I stared at him, stunned. What was he doing?

Then Damien spoke, his voice rough. "I owe you an apology. I should have told you about the snowmobiles. I should have let you know there was an option to leave to help you with your worry about Max."

My breath caught. An apology? Were the four horsemen of the apocalypse riding on the horizon? Had we actually been in Hell this whole time, and this blizzard was Hell freezing over?

Then Damien looked up again. "But I won't apologize for the rest. I cherish every moment we spent together, and I want more. Don't run, Katie. Stay with me. I'll offer you a different position, one that's unpaid, but it'll be permanent. Legally binding, even."

Trust Damien to come up with a way to ask a woman to marry him that mentioned a salary. Or lack of same.

But still, my heart clenched. I wanted to touch him, lose myself in his arms. My inner voice of reason warned me he was used to getting his way. He'd also taken care of me after I crashed and wasn't implying I couldn't leave now. Was I free?

One way to find out.

I steeled myself. "I need to go to Max, Damien. I have responsibilities to Max. He's all the family I have."

Damien's eyes darkened. For a moment I thought he would argue, demand that I stay whether I wanted to or not. Then he squeezed my hand and rose to his feet in a smooth motion.

"You're right, of course. Family should come first, always." His tone was matter-of-fact, but I glimpsed a flicker of something in his gaze I couldn't identify. "If your brother's presence is what you need, then I won't stand in your way. You need to know that my offer remains open and sincere if you change your mind."

My throat tightened at his quiet acceptance. How was it possible to be so torn about wanting to stay and wary about what he might be up to? I didn't know whether to be relieved or bereft, but I did know he had something up his sleeve.

Before I could sort through the tangle of emotions, the doorbell announced an arrival.

I glanced at Damien, who helped me to my feet and held the door for me.

Rico was stamping snow off his feet, a pile of shopping bags next to him, and a shorter slighter figure with auburn hair behind him. A gust of frozen air curled around me as the other person stepped into the cabin.

"Max," I hobbled forward and threw my arms around my brother. Alex, third in line, slammed the door behind them.

Max hugged me back just as fiercely, and the tension eased from my shoulders. He looked tired but fine.

"Surprise," Max grinned at me. "Your boss sent peeps to the apartment, and they offered me a ride up here for Christmas. In a private jet, Kay! Hope you don't mind."

"Mind?" I laughed, blinking back tears of joy. "This is the best gift ever."

From the corner of my eye, Damien watched us.

Despite everything, I felt a flood of warmth and, yes, love at the knowledge that he had arranged this reunion.

I pulled back to get a better look at my brother. "How are you feeling?"

Max waved away my concern. "I'm fine. A little tired, and some new meds, but nothing I can't handle. The trip was super luxurious."

"I'm so glad you're here." I gave him another quick hug. "I was so worried."

"Nice place," Max glanced around the grand foyer. "Quite the place your boss has here, huh? You've been working all this time?"

Heat rose in my cheeks. "Yes, I've been working whenever the lights were on." Twisting the truth wasn't quite a lie, was it?

"Why don't we take your bags up to your room, Max?" Rico said.

"Sounds good." Max grinned, clearly noticing my evasion but letting it slide for now.

As they headed up the stairs, I moved to Damien's side. "Thank you," I said softly. "For bringing him here. It means a lot."

Damien touched my cheek. "I'm glad to do it. Family is important."

"I think, maybe, I'll consider your offer. So long as you think my family is important too."

He kissed me gently. Warmth flooded through me, but Damien pulled back.

"Your poor body needs more rest, and it won't get it if we do that much longer," he said.

I leaned against him. His consideration chased away the last of my doubts and filled me with a deep contentment.

This was shaping up to be the best Christmas ever.

EPILOGUE: DAMIEN

FOUR MONTHS LATER

Steam rose from the cracked door of the bathroom, the scent of Katie's cherry blossom shampoo wafting into the bedroom. I leaned back against the headboard, hands folded behind my head, and waited.

The running water stopped. A few moments later, the door creaked open. Katie emerged, wrapped in nothing but a blue towel and her damp red curls.

My gaze raked over her body, taking in the curve of her hips and the swell of her breasts. Warmth bloomed in my chest at the sight of my mother's wedding ring glinting on her finger, a symbol that she now belonged solely to me and always would.

"Like what you see?" A coy smile played on her lips as she sauntered to the dresser.

I hummed appreciatively, the warmth in my chest sharpening into desire. "Very much so."

She bent at the waist to rifle through her underwear drawer, giving me a tantalizing view of her ass. I gritted my teeth against the urge to drag her onto the bed and take her right then and there. We had all night, after all, and every night thereafter.

Katie straightened and turned, a scrap of red lace dangling from her fingers. My breath caught at the sight of her bare breasts, nipples puckered from the cool air in the room. She slanted me a mischievous look as she slid the lace up her legs and hips, putting on a show.

Heat pooled low in my abdomen, my cock already ready. I rose from the bed and stalked toward her, pinning her against the dresser. Her eyes widened, but a little smile played on her lips.

I grasped her jaw and crushed my mouth to hers, swallowing her gasp. Her lips parted eagerly under mine, her tongue dancing with my own. One hand slid down to palm her plump, full breast, relishing her soft moan.

When we finally broke apart, panting, I nipped at her earlobe and murmured, "What was in that package you got today, *mi tesoro*?"

Katie drew back, eyes sparkling, and reached into the drawer beside her. She withdrew a small white stick and held it out to me.

My heart stuttered, then leaped. A plus sign. A pregnancy test.

Positive.

I stared at the stick, stunned into silence. Then I looked up at Katie. Her lips were curved in a soft, tentative smile and her eyes were suspiciously bright.

"Surprise?" Her voice wavered slightly. She was worried about my reaction.

Joy bloomed in my chest, fiercer and more overwhelming than any other emotion I'd ever had. I crushed her close.

She squeaked in surprise but then her arms came around me in turn.

I kissed her again, deep and thorough, pouring all my emotions into that kiss. By the time we parted, we were both breathless.

"*Ti amo,*" I said fiercely. "I love you."

"I love you too." Her mouth curved. "And I plan to take lessons in Italian, starting tomorrow."

The email alert on my phone cut through the haze of bliss. I reached for the device, intending to silence it, when a familiar voice came through the speakers.

Moretti. Carina and Bria's asshole father. I'd bugged his office, and security had forwarded the recording as urgent. This was probably bad.

Beside me, Katie stiffened, my tension contagious. I squeezed her hand in warning, putting a finger to my lips.

"—have a proposition for you," Moretti was saying, his tone confident, though there was an undercurrent of fear.

A pause. Echoing, probably from a phone on speaker, a gravelly voice responded, "This had better be good, Moretti. I don't appreciate being disturbed."

Romano. The don of the family responsible for Carina and Bria's brother's death. Why was Moretti talking to him?

"I want to make a deal," Moretti said. "You know what I want. I'm offering you something you can't refuse in exchange."

"Oh?" Romano's contempt was clear in his tone. "What could you possibly have that I want, Moretti?"

"My daughter."

***

We hope you enjoyed this start of Marrying the Mob while getting to know Damian and Katie. He's a bit of a rascal, isn't he? There is so much to come in the series and although each is technically standalone, you'll find cameo appearances of our main characters throughout. Who do you think you've met so far in Stranded? As of this writing, four Mafia Boss books are planned (Stranded with, Given to, Protected by and Turning into) but we are open to more if characters start begging to be written...we admit to being a little afraid they won't bother begging and will just "encourage" us at gunpoint!

Ok, back to that ending; which daughter do you think the twins' father was talking about giving away? Bria or Carina? Is he serious? Or is this perhaps a ploy to get to the man who had their brother killed and annihilate him? How could he even consider doing this to one of his daughters anyway? Click below to find out now in Book 2 of Marrying the Mob, Given to the Mafia Boss. We absolutely Can. Not. Wait. for you to meet Luciano. Seriously, just look at his cover!!